AN AJ DOCKER & BANSHEE THRILLER

PHANTOM FILES

GARY GERLACHER

Black Rose Writing | Texas

The author grants the final approval for this literary material.

First printing

This is a work of fiction. Names, characters, businesses, places, events, and incidents are either the products of the author's imagination or used in a fictitious manner. Any resemblance to actual persons, living or dead, or actual events is purely coincidental.

ISBN: 978-1-68513-721-2 Paperback; 978-1-68513-722-9 Hardcover
LIBRARY OF CONGRESS CONTROL NUMBER: 2025945931
PUBLISHED BY BLACK ROSE WRITING
www.blackrosewriting.com

Printed in the United States of America
Suggested Retail Price (SRP) $19.95 (Paperback) 24.95 (Hardcover)

Phantom Files is printed in Minion Pro

*As a planet-friendly publisher, Black Rose Writing does its best to eliminate unnecessary waste to reduce paper usage and energy costs, while never compromising the reading experience. As a result, the final word count vs. page count may not meet common expectations.

For everyone who plays a part in delivering emergency care,
thank you for your service.
BAFERDs, keep BAFERDing!

PRAISE FOR
THE AJ DOCKER & BANSHEE THRILLER SERIES

"Buckle up for another *Doc and Banshee* thriller as they risk everything, including their lives, to foil an international terrorist assassination plot while bringing readers inside the emotional journeys of two families facing unimaginable, life-threatening medical emergencies."
–Bob Rothman, author of *A Terrible Guilt* and, coming in 2026, *The Shark's Protégé*

"A magnetic medical thriller—Gary Gerlacher nailed it!"
–Cam Torrens, award-winning author of the *Tyler Zahn series*

"Book 6 of the AJ Docker medical thriller series lives up to its earlier installments and might just be my new favorite!"
–Lucille Guarino, award-winning author of *Elizabeth's Mountain* and the *Lunch Tales* series

"Caution: *The Phantom Files* is a best-selling medical thriller that may cause readers to experience rapid breathing, heart-pounding, spine-tingling, page-turning excitement."
–Gail Ward Olmsted, author of the *Miranda Quinn Legal Twist* series

PHANTOM FILES

CHAPTER ONE

Monday, 6:00 a.m.

Lenny Nielsen began the last day of his life at exactly six o'clock, when his alarm featured the gentle sounds of a waterfall. A creature of habit, he rose at six daily. After thirty-one years of marriage, his wife didn't even notice, as he slid quietly out of bed and entered the bathroom.

His four-minute shower consisted of three minutes of washing under hot water, followed by a minute of standing under cold water. Thoroughly awake, he brushed his teeth, combed his hair, and walked into the closet. A long line of shirts, pants, and coats hung precisely in a straight line. He hurriedly dressed in a starched, light blue button-down shirt and dark slacks he had set aside the night before.

He checked his appearance in front of a full length mirror. He brushed away imaginary lint and straightened invisible wrinkles in his shirt before reaching for his badge that hung beside the mirror. He glanced at the badge in his hands, "Dr. Larry Nielsen, Md, PhD, Chief of Service Obstetrics and Gynecology at Tempe Memorial Hospital." The nine-year-old picture, taken when he was fifty, reflected the remarkable lack of change in his appearance. His hair was grayer but resisted bald spots. His face featured a few deeper wrinkles, and his belt size had increased from thirty-two to thirty-four inches. Overall, he was in great health due to his strict diet, heavy work schedule, and regular workouts. A person meeting him would most likely describe him as distinguished, a term appropriate for his position at the hospital.

He walked into the kitchen, where Kenzie, his border collie, sleepily greeted him. She had been a rescue and remained a bit neurotic, but she was unfailingly loyal and always rested at his feet while he breakfasted. He quickly prepared an omelet loaded with vegetables chopped the day before, ate a bowl of fresh fruit, and downed a glass of milk. Lastly and most importantly, he sipped his coffee, a special Colombian blend he had discovered years ago and for which he paid an obscene price to ship to his house every month. Any doubts he had about the justification of the expense dissipated, as the rich flavor and caffeine further energized him.

He glanced at his phone to see if the world had managed to survive another day without catastrophe. The news was surprisingly dull, always a good thing. He finished breakfast and placed the dishes in the dishwasher before wiping down the table. On her back with her paws stretched in the air, Kenzie patiently waited for her belly rub. It was all she asked in return for her loyalty, and Dr. Nielsen obliged her with some kind words about what a good girl she was.

He silently said goodbye to his wife and two daughters sleeping upstairs. Years ago, he would have walked upstairs to give each daughter a kiss on the forehead before he left, but they were older now, and that tradition had stopped long ago. He settled for a mental goodbye to them, hoping they each had a great day.

The drive to the hospital was only fifteen minutes at this hour, as opposed to the thirty minutes it would take at rush hour. He spent it in comfort in his Mercedes S Class sedan with the powerful engine moving silently through the dark streets. The seat vibrated in massage function, as he listened to sports radio hosts critique local teams.

He parked in his usual spot and climbed out of the car with a weak protest from his right hip, a reminder of his schedule for the day. He entered the hospital at precisely seven o'clock, and for the first time that day, his routine changed. Instead of turning right to take the elevator to his office, he turned left toward the radiology suite, where a receptionist smiled at him.

"Good morning. I'm Karen. How can I help you today?"

"I'm Dr. Nielsen, here for an MRI of my right hip this morning."

"Of course. All of your paperwork is complete. If you follow me, I'll take you back to Henry, who will be in charge of your scan today."

Dr. Nielsen followed her through a maze of hallways and appreciated their efficiency. She introduced him to Henry before returning to her desk. Dr. Nielsen made a mental note to call out her perfect demeanor to her department head later in the day.

"Good morning, Dr. Nielsen. I'll be in charge of your scan today. If you would please follow me, we will get you started." Henry was a young man in his twenties with an infectious smile and an unruly mop of dirty blond hair. In his scrubs, he looked ready for a sleepover instead of a workday, but he was friendly and seemed competent. Henry led him to a dressing room and handed him a pair of scrubs.

"Everything in the locker. You can keep your underwear and socks on, but nothing else except the scrubs. I'll be outside when you're ready."

Dr. Nielsen changed efficiently, slowing only to make sure there were no wrinkles in his pants or shirt as he hung them, and met Henry outside.

"Have a seat, Dr. Nielsen, and we'll get this IV in place. Have you ever had an MRI?"

"No. I've ordered quite a few, but I've never needed one myself."

"The study should take about fifteen minutes, and then I'll come in and inject the contrast, and we'll get the last set of images. Total time should be about twenty minutes. Just to double check, you have no jewelry or piercings or medical devices implanted on you?'

"No, sir."

Henry expertly slid the IV in place and secured it with tape. The IV and tubing were free of any metal and safe to use in the MRI machine. "Okay, what type of music do you like?'"

"Classic rock."

"Good choice. I've had too many requests for Taylor Swift lately. Classic rock will be refreshing."

Henry led the way into the room, and Dr. Nielsen positioned himself perfectly centered on the bed. Henry handed him an inflatable ball for his right hand. "I don't expect you'll need it, but if for any reason you need me to stop the exam, just squeeze that ball. I'll stop the scanner and slide the table out of the machine. You're not claustrophobic are you?"

"I don't think so."

"It can feel pretty tight in there. I recommend you close your eyes and focus on the music. If you keep your eyes closed, you won't have to experience the small space. Okay, let's get this done."

Henry turned on the music and slid the table into the machine until the hip was situated in the correct spot. Dr. Nielsen took Henry's advice, closed his eyes, and focused on the music. The first song was by Bruce Springsteen, a good omen.

Henry closed the heavy door, sealing the room tightly, and entered the control room overlooking the exam. He double checked that everything was correct, then spoke into the microphone.

"Okay, Dr. Nielsen. We're gonna get started. The machine will be loud, but just sit still, relax, and focus on the music."

Henry triggered the controls to start the machine, and the familiar clanging of the MRI machine reverberated through the control room. He heard an unusual high pitched sound, followed immediately by the patient's alarm from Dr. Nielsen's squeezing the inflatable ball. He looked through the window to see what the problem was and his mind froze, as he tried to process the sight in front of him. It made no sense. It was impossible.

His hand reflexively reached for the emergency stop button, and the machine silenced, but the high-pitched scream continued. Henry managed to push the "Code Blue" button before he violently regurgitated his breakfast.

CHAPTER TWO

Monday, 6:50 a.m.

"C'mon, Banshee. Time for another day at work."

Banshee barked softly and swished his tail, showing entirely too much energy for a Monday morning. A former police dog who had been forced to retire after taking a bullet meant for me, my svelte Belgian Malinois was fearless, loyal, and the best traveling companion I could ever imagine.

As an emergency medicine physician, I travelled the country on three to six-month contracts with hospitals. The opportunity to explore new cities and experience different hospital systems throughout the United States provided fresh adventures. My contract was in month two of a four-month stint at Tempe Memorial Hospital in Phoenix, the largest trauma center in the area.

I slung my backpack over my shoulder and exited the car with Banshee stepping out after me. Under his service vest, he wore ceramic plates stronger than titanium that had saved his life more than once. They had been custom designed by a Chinese billionaire after Banshee helped him recover some stolen jewels.

"What's up, Dr. Docker?" a voice called from behind me. Banshee spun to assess the situation, while I leisurely glanced over my shoulder.

The speaker was a mountain of a man, approaching rapidly with his hands open.

"Come here, Banshee."

Banshee, recognizing a friend, leapt into his open arms and rewarded him with vigorous facial kisses.

"Good morning, Dirk. How was your weekend?"

"Great, Dr. Docker. My soccer team won 3-2 and advanced to the league's finals."

"Congrats, and please call me Doc. Dr. Docker sounds like a stutter. How the hell did they score two goals on you?"

It was a legitimate question. Dirk was the goalie and a huge human being. I'm six-foot-one and 195 pounds, and Dirk was easily seven inches taller and a hundred pounds heavier. He had excelled on the basketball court until college, when three knee injuries within two years ended his athletic career. He pivoted to become a paramedic. He loved the work in the field, but his bulk made it hard for him to work within the constraints of an ambulance. He decided to work full time in the emergency room, and despite having hands the size of Shrek's, he could place an IV in even the smallest patient. Loud, boisterous, and gifted with an infectious laugh that brightened everyone's day, he had an opinion on everything and was unafraid to share it. His kind and gentle nature belied his ability to play the part of an enforcer. One glance at Dirk's towering presence as he administered behavioral correction was usually enough to compel cooperation. He and Banshee had become fast friends, and I suspected that they shared a distant feral ancestor.

"It was a bit embarrassing to let two goals in. I guessed the wrong way on one penalty kick, and I couldn't see the other shot until it was too late." He let Banshee down to the ground. "That dog has some serious jumping ability. How high do you think he can jump?"

"Over you, easily," I said.

"Don't get me wrong. I'm a fan, but are you saying that Banshee can clear almost seven feet?"

"Let's see. Come stand over here."

I positioned Dirk in the grass, then led Banshee forty yards away and had him sit. I returned to stand beside Dirk.

"Do me a favor, take your phone out and hold it next to your head on video. This will be a great shot. Stand still no matter what."

Dirk straightened his back and started his video. I called out to Banshee, "READY."

Banshee remained seated, but visibly tensed, like a race car ready to leave the line.

"JUMP OVER," I said, pointing at Dirk.

Banshee's two back feet dug into the dirt, and his powerful legs launched him forward. His front legs stretched in midair, reaching for the ground to pull him forward until once again his back legs could dig into the dirt to propel him even faster. Within two strides, he moved at over twenty miles per hour toward Dirk. When he was eight feet away, he launched from his back legs and angled upward, flying over Dirk with his legs stretched out in front and behind, clearing him by a good six inches. To Dirk's credit, he didn't flinch. Banshee landed softly on the grass and turned for his next command.

"Relax, good boy." Banshee came over for his well deserved ear scratch.

"Damn. I'll never bet against that dog. Is there anything he can't do?"

"Unfortunately, he can't fill out my patients' charts or do laundry, but he's phenomenally well trained. Come on. Let's get to work."

We badged our way into the emergency department, and I set my things down in my work area. Tempe Memorial Hospital had been around for over thirty years, but had undergone a major rebuild about six years before. The spacious, modern design of the emergency room promised high quality care, and the wide hallways, oversized rooms, and fifteen-foot ceilings avoided the claustrophobic feeling of older hospitals. It was one of the nicest hospitals I had ever worked in.

"Good morning, Sue. How was your weekend?" Sue was the charge nurse for the day. With over twenty years of experience in the emergency room, she had seen almost everything, and no problem was too big for her to tackle. Her quiet demeanor disguised an extraordinary mind capable of deftly handling ten problems at once. With her sandy blond hair that became progressively frizzier as her shift passed, large wire frame glasses, and trademark pen over her right ear, she looked more like a librarian than a nurse.

"Not bad, Doc. Finally got around to closing out some projects that had been hanging over my head."

"Always satisfying to clear up the to-do list. What's the day looking like?"

"Off to a promising start. No one called in sick, which is a minor miracle for a Monday, and we have no holdovers waiting for a bed. So with a full staff and a relatively empty emergency room, I don't expect we'll lose control of everything until at least this afternoon."

"Sue, I have no idea how you're such an optimist after all your years in the emergency room."

"I'm a realist. I know chaos always looms. I just don't know when it will prevail, but hopefully, not until after lunch."

"I'll give you 3-2 odds that it happens before lunch."

Sue shook her head and left to see to her duties, and I logged onto the computer to see that only eight patients occupied beds, and none looked critical. Banshee curled up at my feet, as I waited for the night doctor to finish and check out her patients to me.

An overhead alarm shattered the peace with a mechanical announcement. "Code blue, main radiology, MRI suite one. Code blue, main radiology, MRI suite one."

Banshee abruptly stood at the call to action from the overhead alarm, but I commanded him to stay under the desk. Sue hurried around the corner and motioned for me to follow. "You're up, Doc. We're responsible for code blue calls in radiology."

We fell in behind Dirk, who had grabbed the emergency kit. Although each hospital area was supposed to have a code cart, we always brought essential supplies with us to avoid any potential delays in care. The bag weighed twenty-five pounds, and Dirk shouldered it like an empty backpack.

"What do you want to bet it's an allergic reaction or a fall?" I asked Sue, as we jogged to keep up with Dirk.

"Hopefully, it's nothing too crazy."

Dirk made the final turn ahead, and a radiology technician frantically waved to us. Dirk unexpectedly stopped in the doorway, and Sue and I plowed into his back, which felt like running into a steel wall, and we jolted to a stop.

"What the hell is this?" Dirk asked, as he resumed walking into the room, clearing the way for Sue and me to see our patient.

We paused, as we tried to comprehend the sight. An older man lay on the MRI table, covered in blood, with what appeared to be multiple projectiles sticking out of him. Blood dripped onto the floor and spread in widening circles below him.

We rushed to his side and began our assessment with evaluation of airway, breathing, and circulation. He had an airway, but his ineffective breathing consisted of agonal breaths. Closer inspection revealed that the projectiles were three-inch nails, and at least fifty had pierced his head, neck, and shoulders.

I called for the laryngoscope and breathing tube to intubate him, but Sue had frozen and stared at the patient.

"Sue. Sue! Snap out of it. We need to intubate him, now!" I insisted.

Sue shook her head and started moving, slowly at first, but regained control of herself, as she recovered. "Sorry. I know him. This is Dr. Nielsen, Chief of Ob/Gyn, and he's been my own doctor for years."

I filed that information away along with the thousand other questions I had about how he ended up being stabbed by a bunch of nails in an MRI machine. "I'm sorry. Let's get him intubated and over to the trauma room. Dirk, what do you have down there?"

Dirk, working efficiently, had hooked up IV fluids and a monitor. "I've got a liter of normal saline running full blast with a pressure bag. Pulse is 175 and weak. Not gonna even try for a blood pressure. This guy's about to code."

I agreed. The massive blood loss would kill him soon, unless we could replace it and at least slow the bleeding. I opened his mouth and slid the laryngoscope into the back of his throat. I had to avoid a couple of nails that had penetrated his cheeks, as well as the tip of another visible near his airway. Through a fair amount of blood, the intubation was successful, and a respiratory therapist took over bagging the patient.

"Dirk, grab that end of the sheet and let's move him to the stretcher. We need him in the emergency room for a chance to save him."

Dirk grabbed the lower body, while I grabbed the sheet under his head and shoulders, and we slid him onto the stretcher, leaving a trail of blood. The respiratory therapist took her place at the head of the bed, while Dirk placed the monitor on the bed and grabbed the IV bag. We moved toward the emergency room with a trail of blood marking our passage.

We weren't even out of the radiology suite, when the monitor screamed an alarm for asystole, as the heart tracing flat lined.

"Dirk, begin compressions and keep moving."

Dirk walked alongside the stretcher, placed his massive hand on the patient's sternum, and pressed down as he walked. With the first compression I heard ribs snapping, but Dirk continued pushing down at a rate of one hundred beats per minute. With each compression, fresh blood seeped from the wounds in the neck.

Thirty seconds later, we were in the trauma room, and the team went to work to start a second IV. Two units of blood were hung under pressure bags to both IVs, as CPR continued. Pressure was applied to the areas that were bleeding the most, but the majority of the blood loss came from the neck with no way to compress the area and adequately stop blood flow. Removing the nails was not an option, as it would only increase blood loss.

Our efforts continued for another twenty minutes, but ultimately proved futile. At 7:41 a.m, we stopped, and I pronounced Dr. Nielsen dead. The team stepped back in defeat and evaluated the scene in silence. Dr. Nielsen lay naked on the table, his skin white beyond any natural skin tone, marred by the bright red blood that covered his body like an obscene Jackson Pollock painting. The only sound was the constant drip of blood splashing against the floor.

The nails had pierced him like a pincushion all over his upper body. There had to be more than fifty of them. Some caused only superficial cuts, especially across his scalp, but the fatal damage was to the soft tissue of the neck, where the nails had penetrated deeply into major blood vessels. I picked up a nail that had fallen out during our attempted resuscitation and examined it more closely. Typical three-inch nails, commonly found in every hardware store, had been turned into hideous murder weapons.

I addressed the team. "Thanks for the effort, everyone. Unfortunately, the injuries were too great, and he didn't have a chance. Let's get him covered with a sheet, and make sure to leave everything as is. This is going to be a murder investigation, and we need to leave everything intact for the authorities. Please maintain patient privacy with no gossip about this, especially when the press shows up."

I scanned their stunned faces. They were used to seeing the effects of violence in all kinds of brutal forms, but this savagery reeked of a special kind of evil. A colleague from the hospital had been horrifically murdered in an MRI machine. Even the calloused hearts of an experienced emergency room staff were emotionally unprepared for this kind of cruelty.

I saw Sue in the back of the room with tears pooling in her eyes. She made eye contact with me and immediately turned to leave the room.

"Dirk, please get him covered and secure this room until the authorities arrive. I'm gonna run back to MRI real quick."

"You got it, Doc."

I dropped my gloves into the trash and pulled on some booties to prevent blood tracking all over the place. Banshee watched attentively, as I exited, highly attuned to the presence of so much adrenaline, blood, and drama.

"Here, boy, with me."

Banshee fell in at my side, his nose working overtime to categorize the scents. I didn't have to worry about getting lost, as I followed the bloody trail back to radiology. I arrived at the MRI suite just as Carmen was pushing her cleaning cart into the room.

"Hold up a moment, please," I said.

Carmen turned her attention to me and smiled softly. She was part of the cleaning crew for the emergency room and always offered friendly warmth.

"What are you doing in here?"

"Radiology asked me to clean the MRI room."

"There must be a mistake. We need to keep this room untouched for the authorities. I think they meant they wanted the hallways cleaned."

"They said to clean the MRI room first."

"It's been a chaotic morning. We need to keep this room untouched, so please focus on cleaning the hallways first, and we'll let you know when this room is ready to be cleaned."

"Okay, Doctor. Did the poor man die?"

"Yes, he didn't make it."

"I will pray for him and his family."

One of the many good souls who kept the hospital functioning, Carmen pulled her cart back into the hallway and began to mop the blood off the floor. I stepped into the room for a quick survey before the circus arrived. The bloody table looked like it had suffered through a war zone, and dozens of nails were spread on the table and floor around the machine.

I turned my attention to the perimeter of the room. Three small cardboard boxes did not belong in the room, one directly opposite the head of the machine and the other two on a diagonal line about forty-five degrees from the MRI machine. The three had been positioned to launch their nails toward the machine as soon as the magnet turned on, definitely intentional.

I studied the box at the head of the machine and saw that it sat on a piece of paper. The box partially obscured words printed on the paper. Wearing a pair of fresh gloves, I gently lifted the box to expose the message. I stared at the words in disbelief, as the mystery deepened. I took a picture of the message before returning the box to its original place.

Outside the room, I found a radiology technician bent over, racked with sobbing.

"Hey, man, what's your name?"

"Henry. I didn't know the nails were in there. How could they even get there? He's dead, isn't he? I saw you coding him in the hallway. I can't believe he died!"

Henry was losing it, understandably, given the trauma he had witnessed. "Listen to me. It's not your fault. Someone did this on purpose. You didn't do anything wrong, okay? Why don't you come back with me to the emergency room and step away from here?"

In no condition to argue, Henry nodded. A hospital security guard arrived and peered through the doorway with wide eyes. I reached past him and closed the door. "Officer, please stay here, and make sure no one enters this room or the control room until the police arrive. This area is a crime scene and needs to be processed before anyone else contaminates it. Understood?"

The young officer straightened with his new responsibility and assured me that the room would remain secure. Banshee and I led Henry to the emergency room.

"What do you do now?" Henry asked.

"Make about a thousand phone calls and write up the mother of all incident reports." I left unspoken my growing plans to figure out who had murdered Dr. Nielsen and left that message in the MRI suite.

CHAPTER THREE

Monday, 8:21 a.m.

Banshee and I stopped at Sue's office on the way back to the emergency room. I gently knocked on the closed door and called her name.

"Come in," she stammered.

I found her dabbing her red-rimmed eyes, as she slumped in her desk chair. I quietly closed the door and sat across from her. Banshee, sensing the intense emotions, eased up to her and nuzzled her leg. She appreciated the brief distraction and stroked his head.

"You okay? That hit you pretty hard."

"In twenty years, I have never walked out of a code, but seeing what happened to Dr. Nielsen was too much. That poor man." She held the tissue up as a new round of crying overtook her.

"It's always harder when you know the person. A few months back, I had to take care of my girlfriend's son after his heart stopped at school. It was one of the hardest cases I've ever had to deal with."

"But you didn't walk away from it."

"No, but at the time, no other doctor was available. If there had been, I probably would have turned the case over to them. You stepped away, but we had a full resuscitation team for Dr. Nielsen. It was necessary for your mental health, and the patient's care didn't suffer at all from it."

"Thanks, Doc. Makes me feel a little better. I can't imagine why anyone would do such a horrible thing."

"I can't either. I went back to look at the room and fortunately stopped Carmen before she cleaned it. I found this message under one of the boxes that held the nails. What do you make of it?"

I passed her my phone to show her the picture. The message had been printed on white paper from a black and white printer.

Purification of the hospital has begun.
A price must be paid for past sins.
The Avenging Angel will show no mercy.

Puzzled, Sue reread the message before handing the phone back. "Who the hell is the Avenging Angel?"

"No idea, but I think a lot of people will be working to answer that question. You good? I need to make a few calls, but if you'd like me to stay, I'm happy to."

"I'm okay. Thanks for checking in, Doc. I'll be out in a minute."

Banshee and I strode to the emergency room, where a sense of normalcy had returned. No matter how bad the last case was, the Emergency Department had to keep taking care of the next patient. The staff never had enough time to process emotions, let alone grieve, after trying to repair brutal damage done to people, which explained the high rate of burnout among emergency personnel.

A regular member of the emergency room security team, Officer Tom Hill guarded the door to the trauma room. His bulk and inability to crack a smile resolved most issues before they escalated. In the rare case when a patient chose violence, Officer Hill made them quickly realize that they had chosen poorly.

"I assume you called this in, and the cavalry is on the way?" I said.

"Yes, sir. Circus should arrive within the next ten minutes."

"Thanks. I have one of the hospital security guards watching over the MRI suite."

"I'll send an officer over there as soon as I can. Hospital security is limited to frowning and harsh language. Probably couldn't stop a motivated toddler if they had to."

Hospitals are risk averse, and most have unarmed security personnel who are not allowed to intervene physically with visitors. They generally wear spiffy sport jackets, usually yellow for some unknown reason, and carry only walkie-talkies to call for help. Administrations overlook the irony of calling for help from more people who are not allowed to get physical. In the end, hospital security is nothing more than public relations who help lost visitors find their way.

"Hopefully, they can handle the radiology crowd who tend to be more passive than the emergency room crowd."

Officer Tom rolled his eyes before returning to staring at the wall across from him. He was a patient man until he wasn't. One thing was clear; no one would enter that room without his permission. I returned to my desk to make the call I dreaded.

I was new to this hospital and hadn't interacted with this administration yet, but I strongly suspected that they were all the same. The whole top floor was full of folks in suits making decisions based on financial outcomes instead of on quality outcomes. They knew a lot about PowerPoint but nothing about patient care. They would not like this news at all. I decided to start at the top, as the process would end more quickly that way. I dialed the number and waited for an answer.

"Mr. Gentry's office, how can I help you?"

"This is Dr. Docker in the emergency room, and I need to speak to Mr. Gentry right away."

"I'm sorry. He's busy."

"This is pretty important. Can you please get him on the line?"

"Mr. Gentry does not break his schedule for every doctor that calls. Would you like to leave a message or make an appointment?"

"Sure. Tell him that some lunatic murdered Dr. Lenny Nielsen, the former Chief of Obstetrics and Gynecology, in the MRI suite, and within ten minutes, police and media will be swarming the hospital."

The personal assistant paused. "Is this a joke?"

"I'm afraid not."

"One moment, please."

I listened to peaceful hold music.

"That's an aggressive approach." Anna Guidry, another physician in the emergency room, observed. Only three years out of residency, she looked impossibly young to be a doctor, let alone an attending, but she knew her stuff. Compassionate, kind, smart, and energetic, she had a great career ahead of her.

"A benefit of being a traveling doctor on a short-term contract is that I don't have to concern myself with kissing up to administrators."

"I may have to look into a traveling position."

"It has some advantages, like not having to care who you piss off." I turned my attention back to the phone, as an angry voice yelled at me. Bill Gentry was the CEO of the hospital and not known for his friendliness.

"Who the hell is this?"

Practicing the art of de-escalation, I answered in my most calming voice. "This is Dr. Docker from the emergency room, and there has been an unfortunate incident you need to know about."

"Then call your Chief. Don't bother me."

"Normally I would, but soon, your hospital is gonna be trending on the app formerly known as Twitter for all the wrong reasons. You need to get ahead of this thing quickly." I proceeded to explain what had happened, and to his credit, Mr. Gentry listened without interruption.

"Tell the staff I want a lid on this. No one talks to the press except for our media team. I'll make sure police provide security to lock down the first floor. I need to make some calls." He abruptly disconnected.

"That went better than I expected," Dr. Guidry said.

"Agreed. Who knows, we may even get a pizza lunch out of this mess."

"The ultimate sign of thanks from administration, a hundred dollars worth of pizza for twenty-eight employees with no time to eat."

"You learn fast, Dr. Guidry."

"Do you think his highness will come down and mingle with us common people?"

"He should. Leadership starts with being present, which means it's two to one against him showing up down here."

"Either way, I need to go see some patients. Do you have time later today to talk about something? I have a bit of a strange situation, and I would appreciate your advice."

"I'll make time. We should both be done about the same time today, so we'll figure it out. Right now, I have to go talk to the cops and then figure out who is gonna tell the family. Even for a Monday, this day sucks."

• • •

Officer Hill watched the pair of detectives approach with his signature blank stare. The woman was dressed smartly in a white blouse and a navy blazer, designer jeans and dark designer athletic shoes. Her height and build were average, and her remarkable eyes constantly scanned her surroundings like a hawk hunting for its next meal.

While the woman gave off a serious vibe, her partner resembled a laid back surfer dude. A wrinkled jacket covered his light blue button down shirt, and neither his khakis nor his loafers looked like they were fresh from a wash. Sandy blond hair in an overgrown mess topped off his image. The man was sharing an animated story, as they approached the trauma room. Officer Hill maintained his statuesque pose.

The woman approached until she was uncomfortably close to the officer and looked up to meet his blank stare. "Good morning, Officer Hill. Are you going to move, or do I have to shoot you?"

After a pause Officer Hill peered down at her. "Threatening an officer is a felony offense. You could go to jail for that."

"Lucky for me, you're a lazy piece of shit who hates paperwork. How have you been, Tom?"

Tom flashed a rare smile. "Been doing all right, Detective. So this mess belongs to the First Team?"

"You got that right. They send the best for the biggest cases. Plus, we were on call this morning for the next homicide. Sounds like a bad one," the man said.

"They're all bad. This one is unique. The victim was killed with nails left by the MRI machine."

Officer Hill stood aside and opened the door for Detectives Ellen Frist and Johnny Teamont of the Phoenix police department. Frist and Teamont had worked together for years on the homicide squad and were its most senior detectives. Their nickname of "First Team" was a play on their names and seniority.

"That's a bit of a mess," Teamont said, as they looked at the blood covered room. The once white sheet that covered the body was now stained red, and the nails poking up from underneath gave it an especially ominous appearance.

Officer Hill pointed to the shelf inside the door. "Booties and gloves are there, if you want them."

Frist and Teamont covered their shoes with booties and snapped the gloves in place before they approached the body. Teamont gently lifted the sheet. "I'm no medical expert, but I'm pretty sure that's not a known complication of an MRI machine."

Frist slowly circled the head of the bed, taking in every detail. The man had been in his fifties or sixties and had maintained his physical health. He had an expensive haircut and no evidence of plastic surgery. His tan indicated that he spent some time outdoors, likely exercising. The nails looked ordinary to her at first glance. She tried to imagine the fear and pain of being struck by all of these projectiles at one time. Obviously, the ones in the neck had gone deepest and were likely the cause of death. Frist made a silent vow to find justice for the man before replacing the sheet gently over his head. She snapped off her gloves, as she turned from the body.

"Do we know who he is?" Teamont asked.

"Some bigwig doctor in the hospital," Officer Hill said.

"Who pronounced him?" Frist asked.

"Dr. Docker. He should be over in the charting area. Look for a tall guy with a dog next to him."

"What kind of dog?"

"A bad ass police dog named Banshee. I recommend you make friends with him."

"Thanks for the advice. No one comes in except the evidence team, please. Thanks, Tom."

Hill closed the door, stepped in front of it, and resumed his thousand-yard stare.

Frist and Teamont threw their booties and gloves in the trash and left to find the doctor with a dog.

CHAPTER FOUR

Monday, 9:22 a.m.

"Excuse me. Are you the doctor who took care of the deceased patient in the trauma room?" Frist asked.

I appraised the two people hovering over my work area.

"I'm gonna take a wild guess that you're homicide detectives. I'm AJ Docker, but you can call me Doc. That lazy bum on the floor is Banshee." I stood to shake their hands.

"I'm Detective Frist, and this is Detective Teamont. What does the AJ stand for?"

"I'm afraid we don't know each other well enough for me to share that just yet. Give me a minute to finish this, please."

"You know, we're conducting a murder investigation," Teamont said.

"I'm aware, but I need to write pain meds and orders for the young man in room six who has a broken ankle and needs to get to surgery."

Teamont held his hands up in surrender, as Frist knelt down and called, "Come here, Banshee."

Banshee slowly approached and sniffed her outstretched hand. The scent was new, and he did not sense a threat, but remained wary.

Frist made a sharp movement with her hand held flat out, palm facing the ground. Banshee instantly laid flat on the ground. Frist made a twirling motion and Banshee rolled over and bounded to his feet, excited to show off with the next command.

I finished my chart and turned to Detective Frist. "I'm gonna make another wild guess that you have worked with police dogs."

She pulled Banshee in for a hug and a neck scratch. "When I was on patrol, we had a K-9 unit, and I learned some commands. He's a good boy."

"But not very loyal, apparently." Banshee curled up in her lap. "Let's head to the conference room, where we can have some privacy."

We sat around the conference table, and Banshee stretched out at Detective Frist's feet and gave me side eye.

"Walk us through everything that happened today. Do you mind if we record this?" She asked.

"Feel free to record. We received an overhead call of Code Blue at about 7:10 this morning." I spent a few minutes reviewing everything we had done to try to save the patient.

"Do you remember anything else?" Frist asked.

"Yeah. After I pronounced my patient dead from an obvious murder, I returned to the MRI suite to take another look and make sure that it was secure."

"You shouldn't have gone back there," Teamont said.

"You'll be glad I did, because the cleaning crew was about to destroy your evidence. I asked them to leave and asked a security guard to secure the MRI suite until your team arrived."

"Did you touch anything?"

"No. I didn't touch anything, and I stayed out of the blood splatter on the floor. I did take a quick peek around, and it looks like three boxes of nails had been strategically placed around the room, and one of the boxes looks like it's covering a message."

"A message?"

"Yeah. It's resting on a paper with some words printed on it. I couldn't read it and didn't touch it, but it looked important enough to mention." I figured my insignificant lie would not be discovered, and I didn't want to compromise the case.

The Detectives silently nodded at each other, communicating wordlessly as longtime partners do. "Let's head over to the scene, and you can explain what you saw," Frist said.

They followed me out of the room with Banshee walking beside Detective Frist. I looked back at him and frowned, which he ignored. We found that the security guard had been replaced by a police officer to guard the MRI suite. We pulled on booties and gloves and carefully filed into the room, while Banshee waited outside beside the officer.

The Detectives paused to evaluate the scene with the dried pools of blood on the table and floor, littered with nails. The bloody footprints on the floor gave a sense of the frantic attempts at resuscitation. I stopped in front of the box in the center of the room.

"I assume this is where the nails came from. Similar boxes are there and there, and these boxes serve no purpose in this room. If you look underneath, you can see the paper I'm talking about."

Both Detectives leaned in. Detective Teamont reached with his gloved hand and gently lifted a corner of the box in the same manner I had done earlier. They silently read the message and placed the box back in its original position.

"This just got even more interesting," Frist said.

"Yep. This is gonna turn into a Charlie Foxtrot real quick," Teamont said.

"Doctor, thank you for your time. We would appreciate it if you could keep all of this information quiet while we investigate."

"Of course. Good luck. Hope you find the psycho."

"Will you be around, if we have more questions?"

"I'm working all day in the emergency room, and here's my contact information, if you need me later."

"Thanks. We're gonna figure out who the Avenging Angel is and why they targeted Dr. Nielsen."

"One other thing, Detectives. How do you want to handle family notification? Usually we do it, but I don't want to step on any toes."

"We'll handle family notification. Thanks, Doc."

Banshee and I left them to their plans and headed back to the emergency room.

·   ·   ·

"What's your name," I asked.

"Beckett," replied the young man.

"How old are you, Beckett?"

"Twelve."

"You got a job?"

"No. I'm in school.'

"Being a student is a job. What are you gonna be when you grow up?"

"A professional soccer player."

"You appear to have a good start toward that career." Beckett was in room nine with a wrist injury. He wore a soccer jersey and a baseball hat on backwards. An Ace bandage wrapped his left wrist.

"What happened to the wrist?"

"I hurt it in my game last night. We were tied at one with a few minutes left, and I broke free for the goal. Some loser tackled me from behind, and I landed funny on my wrist. It kinda popped when I fell on it."

"Did you leave the game?"

"No, I took the penalty kick and won the game. Iced it last night, but it hurts more today, and my mom made me come here."

"Congrats on the victory. Let's see what we have here." I gingerly unwrapped the bandage and noted some swelling. I put some gentle pressure on the bones, and he winced when I touched near the joint line.

"Sorry about that. Try this for me. Do it real slow and stop if it hurts. I want you to rotate your arm like this."

I held up my arm, and slowly rotated the forearm back and forth. Beckett copied me, but stopped when he had rotated less than a few degrees. I had him rest his arm back in his lap.

"We're gonna get an X-ray, but I'm pretty sure you have a buckle fracture of the radius. That's the bone that controls rotation in the wrist."

"Is that bad?"

"Not a big deal. It's a simple fracture that heals in about five weeks without surgery. You'll have a cast for a short while, but you can still play soccer."

His eyes lit up when he learned he wouldn't miss any time on the field.

"I have one more important question for you, Beckett. Who's the greatest player of all time?"

Beckett didn't hesitate. "Messi."

"Not Ronaldo?"

"Nope. Ronaldo has more goals, but Messi has more Club trophies, international trophies, and player-of-the-year awards. Messi is the man."

"Hard to argue with that. Sit tight, and I'll get the X-ray ordered."

I went back to my computer, ordered the X-ray, and already felt better.

Sue approached, carrying some bags of IV fluid. "Everything okay, Doc? Looks like the police are finishing up."

"I hope so. Last thing this place needs is more chaos. How are you doing?"

"I'm still pretty shook up." Tears made another appearance in her eyes.

"Hang in there. Shift's almost over."

"Thanks, Doc." Sue left to hang the IV fluids for her patient. I had to give her a lot of credit for hanging in there through the whole shift. Working in an emergency room was tough on an easy day and grueling on the worst days.

Beckett's X-ray showed a simple buckle fracture of his radius, as the exam predicted. I asked Dirk to meet me in the room with some splinting materials.

I entered to hear Beckett detailing for his mom the precise steps needed to perform a bicycle kick.

"Looks like a small fracture that needs a cast, but it should heal within four to six weeks. We'll splint it today and have you follow up with orthopedics in a couple of days."

Dirk walked in with his supplies, and Beckett exclaimed, "Oh my God, you're a giant!"

Dirk was used such reactions, especially when he met kids. "Actually, I'm just a healthy German boy. I think the rest of you are a bit undersized. I heard you're a soccer player. What are your team colors?"

"Blue and red."

"One blue and red splint coming up. Doc told me you think Messi is better than Ronaldo. I assume he didn't hear you correctly."

"Messi is better than Ronaldo."

"Well, in addition to the splint, I'm gonna give you some education on who is really the best of all time."

I left to complete discharge forms, leaving Dirk and Beckett to their argument about the greatest soccer player of all time. Patients like Beckett are a breath of fresh air in the emergency room.

CHAPTER FIVE

Monday, 12:37 p.m.

Comparing notes with Frist, Teamont summarized his thoughts.

"The MRI technician doesn't know anything. He always works Mondays and began his routine exactly as he usually did. He started the machine, heard the screams and alarm, immediately shut it down, and called for help."

"You don't think there's any chance he's our man?"

"Zero. The guy is still shaking, and he puked all over the control room after he saw what happened. His background check is clean. We'll follow up with him again tomorrow to make sure his story hasn't changed, but I don't think he had anything to do with it."

"Okay, what else you got?"

"No cameras cover that MRI suite. We do have cameras in the lobby of radiology, and we'll review those recordings, but four other entrances to that department are unmonitored. Three of them require badges, but the one for the staff from the emergency room is unmonitored and stays unlocked. Anyone with access to the emergency room can get into radiology without identification or cameras."

"So you think it's a staff member?"

"Doesn't have to be. Anyone can put on a pair of scrubs to blend in at a hospital. A fake badge would take only a few minutes to make for someone to become virtually invisible. We'll review all the recordings, of course, from about an eighteen-hour window of when the nails could have been placed, but unless someone strolled in with a weighted down, bright orange bag from Home Depot, I imagine we won't identify any real suspects after we check everyone out. Plus, like I said, anyone could have taken the nails through the entrance intended for emergency staff."

"Anything on the nails?"

"Initial exam reveals nothing specific about them. They appear to be generic three-inch nails that can be bought at any hardware store. Preliminary count is one hundred twelve nails in the room. The lab is gonna take a closer look at metallurgy to see if they can narrow it down, but don't expect any miracles. They will likely be too generic to be of any help other than matching them to samples we find in someone's house."

"I've found nothing useful on an Avenging Angel with my initial search. Nothing in the crime databases, and Google returned about a million search results that don't seem relevant. The IT department is gonna take a deeper dive as well as search the dark web for any mentions. Hopefully, we get lucky there."

"What about the victim?" he asked.

"Dr. Nielsen has been here a long time and was the top dog in the OB/GYN department. People are saying the usual nice things about him, but there's an undercurrent of comments about him being 'very strict,' and the word 'outspoken' was mentioned a couple of times. I got the feeling people weren't completely surprised that someone might target him."

"Then we focus on him and the Avenging Angel, while we wait for the lab and IT to find us something. Let's start with his office and staff and see who might be pissed enough to kill the guy right after we talk to his widow."

"Always the fun part." She sighed.

"Apparently, the CEO already spoke to her on the phone, so at least she is aware of what happened."

"We need to decide what to do about the warning note. This freak has already proved a willingness to kill, and the ongoing threat is pretty clear."

"Threatening, but not specific. We can meet with the hospital's administration and security to determine a suitable plan, but without a specific threat, there's not much we can do. I mean, the note tells us nothing more than the graphic murder already has. Obviously, someone else may be next, but even so, we don't even know if that person would necessarily have anything to do with this hospital."

"Think they'll take it seriously?"

"Given that their head of OB/GYN was executed by nails in their MRI, I would think so."

·   ·   ·

"We're not gonna stop operations because of one death," Mr. Gentry asserted. The emergency meeting of the thirteen board members had been called as soon as news of the note had reached Gentry. Five members were present on video screens, while the remaining eight sat around the oversized mahogany table.

"Another attack would expose us to significant additional liability," Jack Madsen, a retired, highly respected attorney in his seventies and longtime board member, pragmatically pointed out.

Mr. Gentry spoke through gritted teeth. "If we shut down and word gets out about this Avenging Angel, every nut job in the city will be threatening us next week. I say we let the police do their jobs and find this psychopath. In the meantime, we beef up security and continue normal operations."

"How exactly do you propose to secure the building? We have over three hundred patients admitted whose families are visiting. There are two hundred emergency room visits and over a hundred surgeries daily, and that doesn't even count the outpatient visits. Including staff, patients, and visitors, a few thousand people are in and out of the building every day." Mr. Madsen spoke calmly and held the attention of the other Board members.

"It won't be easy, but we will get some resources from the police department to augment our security. We'll increase screening at entrances and limit access into the building through specified doors."

"That will help if the perpetrator is an outsider, but what if it's one of our employees?"

Silence overtook the room, as Mr. Gentry processed that horrific prospect. "What makes you think it's an employee?"

"The killer had knowledge of how an MRI works and knew how to access the suite without detection. It could be a clever outsider, or it may well be an insider."

"I refuse to believe that any of our employees would be involved in murder like this."

"I appreciate your loyalty to the staff, but there are about two thousand employees down there you have never met. Each one of them has their own demons, stressors, and potential mental illnesses."

"This Avenging Angel is responsible. The cops need to find him and shut this down."

The debate lasted another fifteen minutes before a vote was called. Nine of the members, including Gentry, voted to continue normal operations, while four sided with Madsen to limit some procedures until the killer was caught. They turned their attention to detail a plan for the media to frame the murder in a way that minimized damage to the hospital's image.

. . .

Detectives Frist and Teamont finished their initial interviews by three and drove together to meet with the widow.

"We don't really have much to share. We have the bizarre, threatening note left with a prominent doctor killed in a spectacular way. No one saw anything, and the only physical evidence is three cardboard boxes and a bunch of nails," said Frist.

"When you put it that way, we should have it solved within the next few hours," Teamont joked.

"Why do you think they went after that doctor?"

"We need to do a lot more digging, but if you read between the lines, it sounds like he was kind of an asshole. People are usually pretty polite when talking about the recently deceased, and apparently, he wasn't widely loved."

"I'm sure that picture will come into clearer focus over the next few days. Let's see what the wife has to say."

They pulled to the curb in front of the house beside two news vans. They pushed their way through the microphones and muttered "no comment" before they reached the door. A man in his fifties answered their knock.

"We said we're not talking to the media," the man said in a threatening voice.

Frist held up her badge. "I'm Detective Frist, and this is Detective Teamont. We would like to speak with Mrs. Nielsen. Is she available, please?"

The man scanned the badge and stepped aside to invite them inside. "She's in the living room."

"Thank you. And you are?"

"I'm her brother, Don."

They followed him to a large open living room, tastefully decorated with contemporary furniture. Mrs. Nielsen sat on the couch with a young woman on each side of her, presumably her daughters. All three wept, and a pile of tissues littered the coffee table. Mrs. Nielsen rose, as they approached.

"I'm Detective Frist, and this is Detective Teamont. We are sorry to interrupt, but we have a few questions to ask and hope that your answers might help us in our investigation. Is there somewhere private we could talk?"

"Let's head out to the patio. Follow me, please."

She led them through a well appointed kitchen to a backyard that would put some resorts to shame. Boulders accented a large pool, and the sounds from multiple waterfalls masked any noise from surrounding homes. A putting green complete with a sand trap nestled the edge of the pool, and professional landscaping guaranteed privacy.

"This is a beautiful yard," Frist said.

"It's my favorite part of the house. We planted those trees decades ago. Most mornings, I sit out here drinking tea and reading my book."

"Mrs. Nielsen, we're sorry for your loss and hate to intrude on you at this time, but we need to ask some difficult questions to help us find who did this."

"Please, call me Helen. I'm happy to help find this monster."

"Thank you, Helen. Do you know anyone who would want to hurt your husband?"

"Plenty of people probably would want to hurt him, but I don't know anyone who would want to kill him."

"What do you mean by that?"

"How much do you know about hospital politics?"

"Pretty much nothing."

"Hospital politics are a zero sum game. There is a limited amount of power and resources, and all of the departments have to fight for their share. If one department gets more money, then another necessarily receives less. That means that departmental heads battle constantly."

"Where did your husband fit into this?"

"Right in the middle of it. Lenny has been there for over twenty years and outlasted four different administrations. He took his department from a second rate division of the hospital to the second most profitable service line. Only cardiology is ahead of OB/GYN, and he would have passed them within the next couple of years."

"Sounds like your husband was very successful."

"He was relentlessly driven to succeed."

"He must have made some enemies along the way."

"He did, and he didn't care. Anyone foolish enough to stand up to him was usually rapidly swept aside."

"Anyone in particular?"

"No specific names come to mind. After twenty years, I tend to tune out the details. You would have to ask the administration."

"We have a meeting scheduled with them later. Any other enemies or people who might want to hurt your husband?"

"The HOA President hates us, but is too scared to drive down our street. I can't think of anyone else."

They exhausted their list of questions, but produced no new information. After sharing their contact information, the two Detectives left the family to their grief.

"Sounds like ninety percent of the medical staff may be a suspect," Teamont said, as they drove to the office.

"Agreed. What did you make of her? She seemed a little cold. Any chance she did it?"

"There might be a lot of money coming her way, but if she did it, she outsourced it."

"She's on the list for now, but then again, so is most of Phoenix. About the only person I've eliminated as a suspect is you."

"Actually, I don't have an alibi for the time the nails were placed in that room."

"Great. You're on the list as well."

"Maybe he was just a convenient target of opportunity. Maybe it was nothing personal."

"If that's the case, then this is gonna be a lot harder to solve. Besides, the note clearly indicates that he was punished for his sins. We need to figure out what sins he committed."

They drove in silence to the station, thinking of ways they might discover who would want Dr. Nielsen dead and why.

CHAPTER SIX

Monday, 6:47 p.m.

"Doc, you about ready to end this crazy Monday?" Dirk asked.

"I was ready to end this fiasco shortly after I arrived. Thanks for your help today."

"Happy to help. Still trying to figure out why anyone could think it's okay to pincushion a guy with nails. It seems dramatic, even compared to all the other effects of brutality we deal with here."

"That's because you're starting with the false assumption that the murderer is rational. If you start with the given that this killer has suffered a severe mental and emotional break, then this violent crime can make a little more sense."

"Yeah, but I've watched a lot of true crime series. Some of these murderers are really smart and organized and harder to catch. I hope we aren't dealing with one of the smart ones here."

"The smart ones are at least more predictable. What do you have planned for this evening?"

"Not much. Probably gonna catch an old movie on Netflix and try to get my mind off this stuff."

"I'm headed over to PJ's Diner. Want to join me? I just need to finish some charts and talk with Dr. Guidry. Give me about thirty minutes to wrap up."

"Sounds better than the reheated lasagna I would eat at home. I need to finish a few things, too."

I found Dr. Guidry completing charts on the computer next to mine. "Do you still want to talk, Anna?"

"If you have time. It shouldn't take more than five minutes."

We found an empty patient room, and she sat on the stool, while I hopped on the exam table. Empty patient rooms were meeting places of choice for emergency room personnel.

"What's on your mind, Anna?"

"I've found myself in an awkward situation, and I don't know how to handle it. Last week, I saw Dr. Connor, the pulmonologist, in the emergency room. Do you know him?"

"Never met the guy. Pulmonology doesn't spend much time in the emergency room."

"Right. He was my patient for back pain after he had fallen off a ladder while cleaning his gutters. The exam wasn't too remarkable, but he appeared to be in a lot of pain with significant decrease in range of motion. I got an X-ray to make sure that nothing was broken and reassured him that it was only muscular pain that would heal over the next few weeks. I wrote prescriptions for Vicodin and muscle relaxers for him and moved on."

"Sounds like you did the right thing. What's the problem?"

"He called me yesterday asking for refills of his medications. He said the pain was still real bad, and he had used up all of his medicine already. I told him we cannot refill pain meds from the emergency room, and if it was that bad, he should follow up with orthopedics. At that point he became a little bit belligerent and threatening, trying to bully me into the refills. It made me really uncomfortable."

"What did you do?"

"I held my ground and refused, and he ended the call by promising to report my behavior to the Board for my refusal to care for him and treat his pain."

"Not a very nice way to end the call."

"Not at all. I don't want a record with the Medical Board. I've heard nightmarish stories about cases involving them. I think Dr. Connor may have a problem with addiction. He is acting like the other drug seekers we see in the emergency room, and he knows better. He knows he should be following up with a back specialist if his pain persists."

"I agree that he might have a problem. What does his visit history look like?"

"He's had several visits to the emergency room here and at our sister hospitals, all of them for pain related issues. I don't know what to do."

"If you believe he has an addiction, you are obligated to report it to protect his patients."

"Then I'm the bad guy who ruined his career. I would be publicly vilified early in my own career. What if he doesn't have a problem after all?"

"What about sitting down with him to discuss your concerns before you report it?"

"I would not be comfortable with that. His bullying tactics scare me."

"What if I sit by your side for support? We could put Banshee on the other side of you. He tends to keep people in line. I think the best thing to do is talk it out with him before you make a report to see if he can provide a reasonable explanation. If not, you have a duty to report him."

"That sucks."

"Welcome to the big leagues where you get to make the tough decisions. Reach out to him, and set up a time for a discussion, but don't take any abuse from him. I'll be with you the whole time."

"Thanks, Doc."

We left the room, and I finished the last of my charts and gave my three remaining patients to the evening physician. I looked at Banshee, who was clearly ready for dinner.

"C'mon, boy. Let's go find you some chicken."

Banshee leapt up and down at the word, "chicken." I stopped by Sue's office on the way out and found her sitting in her chair and staring at the wall.

"Knock, knock. Okay if I come in for a minute?"

"Of course."

Banshee ran to her side for neck scratches, while I took the seat across from her again.

"You doing okay? No offense, but you don't look so great at the moment."

Sue paused before answering. "Today was one of the toughest days of my life. I'm still shook up."

"It was bad for all of us, but it must have been even worse for you, since you knew him. Hey, Banshee and I are heading next door to grab a quick bite with Dirk. Why don't you join us?"

Sue reflected for only a moment before a brief smile flashed across her face. "I accept. I don't have the energy to cook tonight."

She gathered her things and joined us in the hallway. We walked outside together and turned right toward PJ's Diner, owned by a former nurse, who had wisely recognized a need for fast, convenient, and affordable food near a hospital. Open twenty-four hours a day, the casual restaurant offered a diverse menu of affordable options. The retro décor gave it the feeling of a fifties diner, complete with a functioning jukebox in the corner. The tables were beginning to fill, but we were able to secure a booth along the back wall. Sue perused the menu, while Banshee frantically sniffed the air. Our server approached with glasses of water.

"Good evening, Banshee. I haven't seen you in a few days. Are you ready to order, or do you need a minute?"

Sue handed over her menu. "I'll have a burger, fries, and an iced tea, please."

Dirk ordered next. "I'll have a cheeseburger with everything, an order of spaghetti and meatballs, and a side order of mashed potatoes."

The server smiled, probably used to Dirk's impressive appetite. "And for you, hon? Let me guess, a grilled cheese with fries and another grilled cheese with onion rings, a Diet Coke, and two plain chicken breasts for Banshee."

"You know me too well, Pam. Thanks."

I handed her the menu, and she hurried to fill our order.

"I'm gonna guess you come by here regularly," Sue said.

"What can I say? I'm a bachelor, and they make a perfect grilled cheese sandwich. It's much easier to eat here than cook at home."

"I may have to use that strategy more often myself. Cooking for one isn't worth the effort. Thanks for inviting me. Sorry if I'm not great company."

"No worries. You want to talk about it?"

Sue dabbed at her eyes with her napkin to remove the fresh round of tears threatening to spill. "About twelve years ago, I was pregnant for the first time. Eight weeks into the pregnancy, I developed horrible pain and bleeding. Like all good medical professionals trying to self diagnose, I waited too long to go to the emergency room. By the time I was seen, my ectopic pregnancy had ruptured, and I was bleeding out. Dr. Nielsen was on call that night and took me straight to the operating room. He didn't waste time filling out paperwork and just pushed the stretcher up and grabbed an anesthesiologist in the hallway. His fast actions broke every rule in the hospital, but he saved my life that night."

"Sounds like he did the right thing. Did he get in trouble?" Dirk asked.

"I'm sure someone lectured him and put a note in his file, but he had a lot of influence even back then. It didn't hurt him at all, as far as I know, and probably helped build his legend as a go-getter."

"Have you had much contact with him since then?" I asked.

"Only when I saw him around the emergency room, which was rare. He works on the upper floors of the hospital and rarely visits us common folks."

"What kind of man was he?"

"The first word that comes to my mind is driven. He perpetually focused on his next career goal. His obsessive compulsive tendencies made him very controlling. If he believed he was right, no one could influence him to alter that view. He was a difficult man to work for, because he demanded that his staff match his devotion, but no one could match his level of passion."

"He sounds like a complicated man."

"Definitely. He would break any rule or protocol to save a patient's life, but was a stickler for the rules to be applied to everyone else."

"That sounds a bit narcissistic that the rules apply to everyone but him," Dirk said.

"A bit? He was a full blown narcissist. People tolerated him, though, because he accomplished so much."

Our food arrived, and all three of us stopped talking to dig in. Banshee finished first and successfully begged for fries and some burger to supplement his chicken. Dirk shared nothing, as he cleaned his plates himself.

"I did some checking on you, Doc, when you first got here, and you seem like a guy who doesn't shy away from a challenge," Sue peeked at me, hopeful that she hadn't offended me.

I laughed, as I thought of some of my adventures, probably a little distorted online. "That's a polite way of saying Banshee and I find trouble wherever we go and barely manage to drag ourselves out of it."

"Will you help find the person that did this? Dr. Nielsen, for all his flaws, saved my life. His expertise and passionate advocacy for the highest quality patient care is a terrible loss, and he was forced to endure a horrific death. I don't know where to start to do whatever I can to help him now."

I took a moment to consider my answer. "If it's somebody outside the hospital, we need to leave it to the cops. They have all the resources for this kind of investigation. I'll help you look at potential suspects in the hospital. You've been around a long time and know everyone. If it's a hospital employee, I think we have an equal or better chance of finding them than the cops do. Deal?"

Sue shared her first genuine smile since the morning. "Deal. How do we start?"

"Wait a minute. I want in on this, too," Dirk said.

"Hopefully, we won't need the muscle, but it will be nice to have another mind and perspective. Let me think about it tonight. I don't work until the afternoon tomorrow, but I'll stop by earlier, and we can get started."

She placed a twenty on the table and stood to leave. "Thanks for the company, Doc and Dirk, but I need to get going."

I handed her back her twenty. "This one's on me. I'm gonna hang out for a few minutes to get some ice cream."

"I'll keep you company. I hate to pass up dessert."

Sue left, and I thought about what she had said about Dr. Nielsen. He sounded like a guy who had probably made some enemies, or maybe he got killed only because he was a symbol of an overly micromanaged and onerous department lead. Either way, nothing about his murder made sense. There was probably a reason Dr. Nielsen was targeted, and I was interested in answering that question. I would let the police do their thing, but it wouldn't hurt to nose around on my own.

Dirk and I made small talk until our ice cream arrived, and Banshee helped me finish it. The dog could make a fortune as a beggar. I put my money on the table and was about to stand, when two young men walked in and approached the front register. PJ, the owner, sat there most days, greeting customers and collecting money as they left. Her expression darkened.

"Hold up a minute, Dirk. Something is happening with PJ."

Dirk turned in the booth to observe the front of the restaurant. The two men in their early twenties were fairly muscular and sported low quality tattoos on their arms. Their heads were shaved, and they wore tight muscle shirts advertising a local sports team. They stood out from the regular diner crowd. The first man leaned over the counter, invading PJ's space. She stepped back, shaking her head. He leaned over further, and she held up her hands in surrender. She reached under the counter and handed him an envelope, which he slapped against the counter before turning to leave with it.

I was up and moving with Banshee and Dirk as they approached the front door. I followed them outside and saw them headed toward a black muscle car. I sped up to close the gap.

"Holy shit, is that the new Hellcat?" I asked.

Both men spun and reached for their back pockets, but I ignored them and continued toward the car. "I saw an article about this beast. Over 700HP and 650 pound-feet of torque. Look at this beauty."

I circled the car, whistling at the features and ignoring the men.

"Look at that, Dirk. The new downforce package on this thing is incredible."

Dirk used the distraction to move closer to the men. When they turned away from me, they noticed a very large man standing a few feet away from them. Both men subconsciously leaned back from the threat. Dirk wore a friendly smile.

"I noticed you gentlemen took an envelope from PJ in there. I'd like it back, please." Dirk held out his hand.

"Fuck you, man. It's none of your business. Get out of here."

Dirk took a deep breath and seemed to inflate to an even larger size. "Friend, I am gonna count to one. If you haven't given me the envelope by the time I get to one, I'm gonna take it from you."

The men tried to laugh at Dirk's bold declaration, but silenced when they saw how serious he was. They glanced at each other.

Banshee sensed the tension and looked to me for guidance. I gave a hand signal for him to go to alert status. Banshee focused all his energy on the men, waiting for any threatening move. He would not require further orders to attack.

Dirk smiled, "One."

Both men reached for their back pockets but were too slow. Dirk, moving fast for a man his size, grabbed the arm of the one closest to him and squeezed it tight. He pulled the man toward him and enveloped him in a bear hug, leaving him unable to move and barely able to breathe.

As soon as he recognized the gun emerging in the second man's hand, Banshee launched and crushed his jaws together over the forearm, forcing him to drop the gun. The man's incredulous and horrified expression morphed into the shock of pain, as he processed the growling beast clamped onto his arm.

I called off Banshee, grabbed the gun from the pavement, and ordered the man to get down on the ground. Dirk forced his man to sit next to his friend and relieved him of his gun and the envelope of cash.

I told Banshee to guard, and he stood over the men's heads, as a low, constant growl emanated from his throat. Wisely, they remained still.

I called 911, and police officers quickly converged on the scene. I left the weapons on the ground out of the men's reach and calmly answered questions about what had happened. Initially skeptical, the officers checked security footage from inside and out and questioned PJ, who corroborated our story. It turned out that the men had been threatening PJ for months and forcing her to pay an increasing security fee. Soon, the police hauled them away, and Dirk and I were free to go.

"Thanks for the excitement, Dirk."

"No problem, Doc. We make a pretty good team, and I'm glad to work with Banshee, too. I don't mind a fight, and Banshee is a bad ass dog."

"He's a loving, friendly boy until he isn't. Get some rest. Tomorrow we'll start looking for the Avenging Angel."

"Good night, Doc. Good night, Banshee."

Dirk walked toward his truck, leaving Banshee and me alone in the lot. "Think we can make it home without any more drama?"

Banshee leapt into the air, apparently excited about the prospect of more drama.

CHAPTER SEVEN

Monday, 8:53 p.m.

I leaned into a lawn chair on the back porch with a glass of iced lemonade and watched the smoldering sun set over the Camelback Mountains. A dry breeze kept the temperature in the high seventies, and I thanked myself for the foresight to avoid Phoenix in the summer.

Banshee, after completing his inspection of the yard's perimeter, sat like a sphinx next to me to chew a bone. I stroked his ears and welcomed the peaceful end to an awful day. I took advantage of it to collect and analyze my thoughts.

The Nielsen murder had been horrific, but the trauma team's response had been routine. We saw the damage of terrible trauma frequently in the emergency room and compartmentalized it to enable us to handle it effectively, mentally and emotionally. These experiences may have calloused us, but we could never become immune to them. Stressful thoughts and intense emotions had to be confronted eventually to maintain sanity. My eroding expectation that hospitals are a place to heal and to help admittedly triggered my own trauma of witnessing horrific violence in the emergency room where I had last worked. The safety of my medical home turf felt threatened, which made me want to defend it, maybe to heal myself.

I decided to learn what I could about people in the hospital who might have had reason to harbor a festering grudge against Dr. Nielsen, while leaving the investigation of people outside the hospital exclusively to the police. People generally spoke kindly of the dead, but I still got the impression that Dr. Nielsen had offended a lot of people.

The Avenging Angel pointed to another avenue to pursue. A Google search produced an overwhelming number of hits, but I had an easy way to do a deeper dive on the web and searched my contacts. After the third ring, she answered, smacking on gum, as usual.

"What's up, Doc? Been a while. Are you getting into trouble, again?"

"No more than usual. How are you, Spike?"

Spike specialized in searches of the dark web and could hack into specific systems. She lived somewhere in Texas and could access information within a few minutes that would take me weeks to discover, if I could do it at all. Plus, she gave me good prices as a repeat customer, and she and her boyfriend, a fellow hacker, were fans of Banshee.

"Staying two steps ahead of the Feds and making a living. How's Banshee?"

"Happily staying out of trouble, too, mostly."

"Good to hear. What do you need me to break into today?"

"Someone killed a doctor in my hospital today and left a note from Avenging Angel. Google gave me a million useless hits. Could you please do a deeper dive and see if that name has been associated with any other murders?"

"Easy enough. Anything else?"

"Yeah. Please take a look at the victim, Dr. Lenny Nielsen, to see if there is anything unusual on him. The message mentioned 'sins of the past'."

"Everyone has sins in the past, but I'll see if I can find anything interesting. Give me until tomorrow morning, and I'll send you the bill then, too. Make sure you pay me before you start looking into this stuff. Things tend to go sideways when you start getting nosey."

"I'll make sure you get paid before I get arrested."

"Don't say the A word around me. I was referring to your senseless disregard for risking your life. Take care, Doc. Hug Banshee for me."

I ended the call and set my phone on a side table beside my now watered-down lemonade and idly scratched Banshee's ears. Although I watched the stars awaken in the crystal clear, dusky sky, I felt well aware of formidable storm clouds that could be building beyond the horizon.

CHAPTER EIGHT

Tuesday, 7:03 a.m.

The first rays of light peeked through the curtains to wake me and Banshee, lying on the bed next to me with all four legs in the air and his tongue lolling out the side of his mouth. He didn't look like much of a warrior first thing in the morning. I threw on some shorts and a t-shirt and toasted some frozen waffles while I fried eggs for breakfast. I grabbed a Diet Coke and returned to the back porch with my iPad.

Unsurprisingly, Spike's information had arrived in my inbox at three o'clock in the morning. I wondered if Spike slept during the day or was one of those rare people who didn't need much sleep. I made a mental note to ask next time we talked.

Her search on Avenging Angel had led nowhere. A few movies carried that name, but I didn't think an old horror movie with a 33% Rotten Tomato score seemed relevant, but to be thorough, maybe I would have to endure it. A list of books with titles including the phrase also appeared irrelevant, but I couldn't know without reading them. Spike had highlighted her final entry on her list that referenced the Bible. The Avenging Angels, otherwise known as the angels of Vengeance, were the first twelve angels created by God and were associated with the role of punishing wrongdoers. That got me no closer to an identity, but it did provide possible insight into the killing.

The information on Dr. Nielsen was likewise generic and largely useless. Financially, he possessed a level of wealth appropriate for a man with his career, and I detected no evidence of financial impropriety. His life insurance policies had terminated two years earlier, and I saw no financial motive for his murder. Besides an early censure from the Medical Board for unprofessional behavior, his academic career had been a story of success. He had held seats on the boards of a couple charities and overall, he seemed to have lived an orderly, predictable life.

I closed the email and considered next moves. My gut feeling was that somebody in the hospital was responsible for his death. He had spent most of his time at work, and the murder required some knowledge of hospital practices. My next stop would be Human Resources to see if I could get any hint of controversial behavior or even a list of potential enemies. I would need Sue to open that door for me.

Banshee was finishing up his destruction of a fair sized branch. I should have paid attention and given him something nutritious to chew. "What do you say, boy? Ready to go to work?"

Banshee barked softly, ready for the new day.

· · ·

Detectives Frist and Teamont sat to update Lieutenant Jones, a fair, competent leader, but not destined for greatness. He had been around long enough to know how to keep his head off the political chopping block and wanted a quick resolution to the case.

"Good morning. Are you here to tell me you solved it and are ready for your next case?"

"I wish it were that easy, Lieutenant, but this one is gonna take a little longer," Frist said. She opened her notebook to start. "This Avenging Angel moniker is a dead end at the moment. We found no links to any past crimes and no chatter on the internet before this murder. The note the killer left is clean with no prints, and nothing about the ink or the paper is useful."

She flipped to the next page. "We collected one hundred twelve three-inch generic nails that could have been picked up from any home improvement store with no way to tell if they were bought last week or years ago. The boxes are likewise generic with no prints."

"You two don't seem to have a damn thing, but not for lack of effort," he nodded at them.

"Unfortunately, that's an accurate assessment of exactly where we are. We're focusing on Dr. Nielsen to see if we can find a reason he might have been targeted. He was a bigwig at the hospital and had been there a long time. He apparently stepped on a lot of toes in his rise to the top."

"Did he step hard enough to have someone unleash a wave of retribution?"

"Not that we have found so far. His issues seem to have been minor disagreements among academics and nothing that might incite such a brutal response."

"How many people knew he was gonna be in the MRI at that time?"

"The circle of people with that knowledge is relatively broad. His family and staff knew, and everyone working in radiology that day knew that a VIP was coming. Everyone with access to his insurance information could have been aware of it, as well as everyone with access to the hospital system. Anyone who could get into the hospital's computer system could look at the schedule to see who was coming at what time."

"Any way to track who looked at the schedule?"

"The IT people say no. It's a generic feature that can be pulled up from any computer logged into the system."

Detective Teamont chimed in. "We need to figure out if Dr. Nielsen was the target, or if he was the unlucky guy getting the first MRI of the day. The nails had to be set up ahead of time to impale the first person to get a study that day. Maybe he was just unlucky."

The Lieutenant thought through the scenario. "That's certainly possible, but unlikely. What are the odds the attack randomly selected one of the senior doctors in the hospital? Too much of a coincidence, and in homicide, there are no coincidences. Let's tear this guy's life apart and find out who might want to kill him. What are we doing about security at the hospital?"

"The hospital has increased its staff and hired private security to augment it. We have a presence at all the doors, but it's impossible to lockdown the building. Thousands of employees, patients, and families come in and out each day. We don't have the bandwidth to screen all of them effectively."

"We need to prevent another attack. That note certainly threatened one. I like your plan to focus on the doctor and find this maniac before he strikes again. Dismissed."

Teamont and Frist left the Lieutenant's office already contemplating their day of interviews.

•   •   •

Banshee stuck his head out the window and wildly sniffed the wind, as if he were frantic that he might miss a new scent. I parked in the lot, and Banshee seemed to smile when he finally turned to me to lead him inside the cafeteria to meet Sue. Already past the breakfast rush, she waited at a table in a quiet corner, where no one could overhear us.

"Good morning, Sue. Did you get any sleep last night?"

"A little, but I drank a glass of wine and finally took Ambien. Fortunately, it was enough to keep my nightmares at bay."

"Who do you want to talk to first? This is your territory, and you know the people here best."

"I thought about it last night, and I think we need to start in Human Resources. Chuck Damon is the head of HR and has been here even longer than I have. He knows a lot of people, and he would know about any potential scandals."

"How well do you know the guy?"

"We're not close friends, but we've suffered through the same meetings and administrations together for the last two decades. We have what I like to call a survivor's bond which allows a level of trust. Worst that can happen is he refuses to talk to us."

"Let's head up to his office and see if he will tell us what he knows."

Human Resources was located upstairs with all the other administrative teams. Their offices consisted of a sea of cubicles with a row of private offices lining two of the windowed walls. Mr. Damon occupied a large office in the corner. We walked through the cubicles with Banshee, who received inquisitive smiles from the employees. He dutifully strolled past, like he had an important job to attend to.

"I don't think they get many visitors up here," I said.

"Definitely not the four-legged kind."

Sue knocked on the frame of the open door to the brightly lit office. "Hey, Chuck, you got a minute?"

A genuine smile reached his eyes. "Sue, good to see you. Come on in. Who else do we have here?"

"This is Dr. Docker, one of the emergency room physicians, and his service dog, Banshee."

Chuck gripped my hand in a firm handshake. "Nice to meet you, Doc, and nice to meet you as well, Banshee. What can I help you with today? I have about ten minutes before I have to meet with a couple detectives."

I closed the door behind us, and we sat in surprisingly comfortable, upholstered gray chairs positioned in front of his desk. "We're here about Dr. Nielsen's murder, probably the same thing the detectives want to ask about," Sue said.

Chuck leaned back in his chair. "What exactly is your interest in this?"

"Dr. Nielsen saved my life a few years ago, and I've always felt so grateful for that. Yesterday, when we responded to the code in the MRI and saw him bleeding out on the table, it was too much for me. Doc and I were part of the team that tried to save him." Sue's eyes watered, and Chuck gently pushed a box of tissues her way.

"I heard it was horrible. Sorry you guys had to see that, but that doesn't answer my question. Why are you looking into this?"

I leaned forward. "Sue asked me to help her take a look at who might do such a thing. She figured we know the people in the hospital, and if the killer is an employee, we might be able to figure it out more quickly than the police could."

Chuck tapped his pen on his black leather desk blotter, as he looked back and forth between us. "I did some research on you, Doc, before we hired you. You've endured considerable violence at your previous jobs, including bombs, murders, theft, terrorism, and something in Washington that was clearly redacted."

"Trouble does seem to find me."

"That it does. I'm not sure I want to be trending on social media."

"It's a little late for that. Yesterday's murder made it to the top three."

"What exactly are you looking for?"

Sue spoke up. "We want to know if there were ever any threats against Dr. Nielsen. I know he has pissed off a lot of people over the years, but none of those would rise to the level of motivation to kill him. Is there something serious buried in the Phantom Files?"

"What are the Phantom Files?" I asked.

Chuck scoffed and slapped his hands on the desk. "The Phantom Files are only a myth made up by paranoid employees looking for a good conspiracy. Rumor has it these files contain all sorts of sordid details about horrific scandals in the hospital over the decades. It's a neat story, but they don't exist."

"If they did exist, who would have access?"

"They're called the Phantom Files for a reason. I imagine the Chairman of the Board would have access to them and possibly the CEO would, too. Like any big organization, we've had our share of bad actors over the years, but all of them are documented in the system and kept secure to protect the privacy of those involved."

Sue changed tactics. "If there are no Phantom Files, can you at least tell us if there were ever any threats made against Dr. Nielsen, and do you know of anything that might inspire someone to murder him?"

"Like I said, those files are confidential, and I can't share that kind of information, but I can tell you this. After the detectives reached out to me, I reviewed everything we have on Dr. Nielsen and found nothing like that. There's nothing in our files that could possibly justify his murder and that is what I am about to tell the detectives."

Sue rose from the chair. "Thanks for your time, Chuck, and for that reassurance. Hopefully, the police will figure this out."

Chuck mentioned how it was good to see us and shuffled us out the door as diplomatically as possible. We passed the two detectives in the hallway, as we were leaving the department. "Good morning, detectives, any progress on the case?" I asked.

"We have a full list of people to interview today. We'll find him," Teamont said.

We nodded, as we passed them and stepped into the open elevator.

"I don't think the detectives have any idea who did this," I said.

"I agree. What did you think of Chuck?"

"Seems like a nice guy, but he lied about the files."

"How do you know?"

"I'm an emergency room doctor. People lie to me all the time, which has honed my BS detector. I bet those files do exist and that something in them might explain why someone might want to kill Dr. Nielsen."

"What can we do about it?"

"I'm gonna find those files."

CHAPTER NINE

Tuesday, 2:47 p.m.

"Good afternoon, Dr. Guidry. Everything under control in the emergency room today?"

"For the moment, but it's only a matter of time until entropy encroaches and chaos rules."

"So young and yet so pessimistic. What are they teaching young doctors these days?"

"Not the truth. I've learned the hard way from the actual battles in the emergency room."

"Glad you paid attention. The real world doesn't have much to do with the academic world. Any word from Dr. Connor?"

"I left a message for him but haven't heard back yet."

"Then the ball is in his court, and we'll wait to see how he responds. In the meantime, I'm gonna go see some patients."

My first patient, a forty-eight-year-old man with back pain, didn't seem too exciting. The nurse taking care of him gave me a heads up.

"Be careful. He's a farmer."

"On his own or did his wife make him come in?"

"She's at his bedside."

Worst case scenarios scrolled through my mind. Farmers are a different breed of human in that they seem to be the toughest people on earth and tend to avoid hospitals, usually visiting the emergency room only when their spouses coerce them to come, and even then, they downplay their symptoms.

"Good afternoon, Mr. and Mrs. Hirst. I'm Dr. Docker, and I understand you have some back pain."

"I've had back pain for the last thirty years. I don't know why she thinks I need a doctor today."

The woman slapped his arm. "Doctor, don't listen to this stubborn fool. Something is seriously wrong with him."

My usual questions about injuries elicited no significant history, but his back pain did concern me. He had experienced sudden onset of significant pain without an injury, and after I pressed him about it, he admitted to some shortness of breath and nausea. Exam revealed his skin to be cool to the touch, and he had slightly decreased pulses in his right leg. Alarm bells reverberated in my head.

"If I take some aspirin, I'm sure it will be fine in the morning."

"I don't think so, Mr. Hirst. Your history and physical are very concerning for a dissecting aortic aneurysm."

"A what?"

"A dissecting aortic aneurysm. It means that the big artery that carries blood to your lower body may be tearing and leaking blood into your abdomen."

"Is it serious?"

"Yes, we need to get some labs and a CT of your abdomen. The vascular surgeons will come by to speak with you, and you may need surgery this afternoon, depending on what we find."

"Any chance I can go home and schedule it for next week?"

"No, sir. If that aorta is leaking, there won't be a next week for you without surgery today."

"Okay. Do what you gotta do, Doc. I'm just gonna sit here and listen to my wife tell me how she is always right."

"She certainly was right to get you here. She probably saved your life."

"I'm sure she'll remind me of that every day." He squeezed her hand, which she seemed to know meant that he appreciated her. They shared a moment of mutual understanding that they'd always take care of each other.

A quick CT scan confirmed a large aneurysm with some leakage. The cardiothoracic team descended on him, prepped him for surgery, and wheeled him to their operating room inside a half hour.

"Good call on the farmer alert," I mentioned to his nurse, "I don't think I've ever discharged a farmer whose wife made him come in."

. . .

Detective Teamont yawned, as he closed his notebook. "If I have to interview one more person who says that Nielsen was really smart and a pretty good guy, but kind of an ass, I'm gonna look for a security job at a mall. I got nothing to work with."

"Me neither, and the clock is ticking." Both detectives knew that the odds of solving a homicide decreased after forty-eight hours and that key window was closing.

"Did the autopsy show anything?" Teamont asked.

"Nothing helpful. Lots of superficial injuries, and the nail that killed him was directly through the carotid. If that one had missed, he may have survived the attack."

Teamont shuddered, as he thought about recovering from that kind of injury. "I'm not sure enough therapy exists to get a person past such a thing."

"I have a sickening feeling that we're gonna hear from our psycho killer again soon," Frist said.

"Unfortunately, I think you're right."

CHAPTER TEN

Tuesday, 6:14 p.m.

The note, fresh from the printer the killer had purchased six months ago at a garage sale for cash, rested on the meticulously clean, black-finished desk in front of him. Neither the paper nor the printer could be traced to him. He had never touched the paper without gloves, and the printer tray had already been fully loaded with paper when he had bought it.

The other objects on his desk were equally sterile. A stun gun, bought with cash legally from another garage sale in New Mexico, was also untraceable to him, although its original owner might face some interrogation by the police. The needle and syringe were from the hospital's supply of literally thousands and could be from any of its departments. The last object on the desk had been the most difficult to obtain, a bottle of fentanyl. The controlled substance stayed in a locked cabinet with nurses on each shift routinely counting it each day. Stealing the bottle of fentanyl required access he lacked, but he had overcome the obstacle. Someone with access had accomplished the theft, and the killer had taken the bottle from her. The original thief could not complain that someone had taken their stolen fentanyl. The bottle was easily traceable, but not to him.

The killer opened the bottle and inserted the needle, while turning it upside down. He injected some air into the bottle, then slowly withdrew the plunger, drawing all ten milliliters into the syringe and carefully capped it. He held it up to the light to admire the clear, deadly fluid. With over one hundred times the potency of morphine, the small syringe held more than a lethal dose. He placed the syringe, the empty bottle, the stun gun, and the note into a plastic bag, sealed it, and carefully tucked it into his own generic messenger bag. He peeled off his gloves and threw them in the trash, as he double checked his work area to make sure he had not dropped anything. He was ready.

CHAPTER ELEVEN

Wednesday, 5:00 a.m.

Dr. Janet Waverly always began her day with a mug of black coffee. An anesthesiologist, she was used to early working hours. Usually, she took care of her last appointments by early afternoon. Surgeons preferred early start times, and her first case was scheduled for seven, a hip replacement expected to be uncomplicated for an otherwise healthy fifty-five-year-old man.

She tapped her phone to play music through her Bluetooth sound system while she got ready for work. Her husband, a hospitalist, had overnight call and would end his shift as her first case began. He covered nights five days a month, but otherwise, he maintained a schedule more compatible with hers.

She was out the door within forty-five minutes, and her low heels clicked against the clean, white tile in the hospital's quiet hallway at six. Most of the day shifts would start at seven, and she appreciated not having to accommodate the bustle of the changing shifts. She took the elevator alone to the third floor and stepped into the work area reserved for the anesthesiologist. As a senior physician, she had been given a private office, a nine by nine sterile cube, but it allowed for a little privacy throughout the day.

She opened her door and reached for the lights, kicking the door shut behind her, and 50,000 volts pulsated through her body. She stiffened and collapsed onto the floor, landing on her back. She stared at the ceiling, as her desperate mind tried to process what had happened. Her muscles were frozen, but she could hear someone in the room with her. She tried to scream, but those muscles wouldn't work either.

The man tied a tourniquet around her upper arm, then gently turned her arm to evaluate her veins. Dr. Waverly was thin, and a prominent blue vein contrasted with her pale skin. He slid the needle into it and pulled back slightly. A drop of blood entered the syringe, confirming that the needle had been properly placed. Without hesitation, the killer pushed every drop of the fentanyl into her vein.

Dr. Waverly felt the needle puncture her skin, but didn't realize its significance. Warmth flushed through her body, making her lightheaded and then euphoric before she felt utter nothingness. No bright lights or final memories marked her passing. She simply ceased to exist, as the overdose roared through her body.

The killer dropped the stun gun at her side and left the needle dangling from her arm. He placed the note on her chest, aligned it perfectly with the length of her body, and left the empty bottle of fentanyl on top of the paper. He brushed some hair from her face, like a parental caress. He checked for pulses and found none. She looked happy and at peace. Not a bad way to die, he decided. Certainly more pleasant than being stabbed by a hundred nails in an MRI machine.

He peeked into the hallway. This was the moment of maximum exposure. If someone saw him leaving her office, the game would be over, but the odds were in his favor, and the hallway remained empty. He confidently strode to the stairs down to the first floor and stripped off his gloves on the way. He stopped to buy a coffee and threw his gloves into the trash with a napkin before heading to his office. He looked like everyone else dressed in scrubs and headed to work.

• • •

"Where the hell is she? I've got another case after this and a full afternoon clinic." Dr. Noble, like most orthopedists, lacked patience.

The circulating nurse for the operating rooms started calling. Dr. Waverly failed to answer her phone and pages, unusual for her. Finally, she called the department supervisor, who assigned an on-call anesthesiologist to the case, and the hip replacement began only a few minutes late. The supervisor had a break in her schedule and stopped by Dr. Waverly's office. Seeing a light on, but with no answer to her knocks, the supervisor opened the unlocked door. Her screams could be heard two departments away, but were shortly drowned out by the overhead call of Code Blue.

CHAPTER TWELVE

Wednesday, 7:11 a.m.

I had barely settled into my chair to check an overnight patient's lab results, when the overhead call came, "Code Blue, anesthesia offices, Code Blue, anesthesia offices." Sue's eyes conveyed frightened concern from across the emergency room, and I imagine that my own expression mirrored hers. We hustled after Dirk and arrived to chaos in the anesthesia department. Medical professionals and staff milled about, many of them weeping. They opened a path that led us to the office where everyone looked away. Inside, a doctor performed CPR on a woman sprawled on the floor.

I took control of the airway and intubated the patient, as Dirk relieved the other doctor to continue the compressions.

"I found her unresponsive on the floor with a needle in her arm and a bottle of fentanyl on her chest. No pulses present," she informed us.

"Sue, push naloxone IV." Used to treat opioid overdoses, naloxone can have a dramatic effect if given in time. Sue pushed the medicine through the IV she had already placed. I halted CPR to check for pulses, but she remained in asystole. We continued resuscitation efforts for another fifteen minutes before I pronounced her dead.

"Thank you, everyone. We need to leave everything in this room and wait for the detectives. Please don't take anything out of the room or touch anything."

I looked around and made a mental note of a stun gun, the bottle of fentanyl, and a note. I quickly captured a picture of the note before exiting the room and closing the door. I asked everyone to clear the area to preserve what was left of the crime scene for the police.

"Do we know who she is?" I asked.

"That's Dr. Waverly, Department Co-chair for anesthesia," Sue said.

"Another senior physician. I need to make some notifications." I handed Sue the card Detective Teamont had given me. "Would you please call him to let them know what happened? I'll call admin."

"Okay, but someone needs to find her husband, too. He's a doctor on staff here who covers the inpatient units."

I took a deep breath, as I steeled myself to speak to her husband. "Sue, please call admin after you talk to the police. I'll try to track down her husband."

I called the hospital operator and asked for the cell number for Dr. David Waverly. I found a quiet, empty room and called the number. He answered on the second ring.

"This is Dr. Waverly."

"Hello, this is Dr. Docker from the emergency room. Are you in the hospital?"

"Yes, but I am going off service, if this is about a new admit."

"No, I don't have a new admit, but I need to speak to you urgently."

"What is this about?"

"I'll tell you when I get there. Where are you?"

"I'm at the nurse's station on the fourth floor."

"I'll be there in two minutes." I ended the call before he could protest. "Dirk, please keep everyone out of this area until the police take over."

"Yes, sir." Dirk stood with his arms crossed in front of the entry. I felt confident that the scene was secure.

I rushed up a flight of stairs and hurried to the nurse's station. A physician, who I presumed to be Dr. Waverly, stared at me, as I approached, probably trying to figure out who I was. An average-sized man in his forties with the messed up hair and tired look of someone completing a night shift, he wore a Notre Dame sweatshirt over his wrinkled scrubs. I hoped he'd had a chance to rest for at least a few minutes during his shift, since he probably wouldn't sleep peacefully for a while.

"Dr. Waverly?" I held out my hand, as I approached.

"Yes. What is this about?"

"Let's head into the break room to talk." Thankfully, the room was empty, and I closed the door behind me. Dr. Waverly remained standing.

"Dr. Waverly, there is no easy way to say this. I work in the emergency room, and we were called to a code in the anesthesia offices. We arrived to find CPR in progress on a woman in one of the offices. We intubated and attempted resuscitation for over twenty minutes, but we were unable to get pulses back. I pronounced the patient deceased, and the staff informed me that she was your wife."

No matter how many times I tell someone that their loved one is gone, it never gets easier. Everyone reacts differently with tears, anger, fainting, screaming, denial, or in the case of Dr. Waverly, shocked disbelief. He slowly sat in a chair, as his gaze centered on something far away, and he withdrew into his own thoughts. I sat next to him and let the silence continue.

"I don't understand. You said that Janet is dead? She was forty-one and in perfect health. How can she be dead?"

"We don't have all the information yet, but it does not appear that her death was due to natural causes."

"She was murdered?"

"It looks like the same person who killed Dr. Nielsen on Monday may be responsible for this death, too. A similar note was left at the scene."

"How? How was she killed?"

"As you know, it's too early to say for sure, but it may be a fentanyl overdose. The people who found her said there was a bottle of fentanyl in the room along with a needle in her arm."

Dr. Waverly processed that information, and he let his tears fall freely to rain circular stains on his scrub pants. I sat there with him, and after a few minutes, he turned to me.

"I need to see her."

"I can take you down there, but I'm sure the police are here by now. It will be their decision when you can see her."

"Let's go."

He followed me to the elevator like a zombie. His life was forever changed, and I would always be the face of his grief.

The anesthesia offices had been cleared of everyone except Dirk and Sue, and multiple officers had set up around the perimeter, guarding against a threat that had already come and gone. The detectives turned their attention to me, as I entered.

"Detectives, this is Dr. David Waverly, the victim's husband. He is a physician on staff here, and I have given him a broad outline of what happened."

Frist and Teamont exchanged a look that revealed their annoyance with me before Frist took Dr. Waverly's arm. "Come on over here please, and let's talk for a moment."

"I need to see her."

"Sir, this is an active investigation."

"I need to see her."

"Okay. You can look inside the office from the door, but you can't enter the room until the evidence team is done processing it."

We watched, as she led him to the doorway, his gaze averted until the last moment, when he forced himself to face the incontestable reality. Sobs escaped him, and he called her name. Frist gently led him away to a conference room.

"Looks like our killer struck again, Detective," I said to Teamont.

"What makes you so sure?"

"Senior physician, needle in the arm, bottle of fentanyl, and a note, not to mention the stun gun left in the room."

"Stun gun?" He had not gotten a full report yet and had left the room undisturbed.

"Yep. There's a stun gun next to her. My guess is that he zapped her when she walked into the room and then injected her with the drug. If he used the whole bottle, death would be almost instantaneous."

"I haven't seen the note yet. What does it say?"

I opened my phone and displayed the picture for him.

The cleansing continues.
The Avenging Angel wipes evil
From these hollowed grounds.
The purification proceeds.

"That should not be on your phone," Teamont said.

"I'll erase it when you're done with it."

Teamont waved his hand dismissively. "We got a real nut job on our hands. This one was up close and personal."

"But it was also more peaceful than Nielsen's death. Fentanyl overdose beats nail impaction by a few orders of magnitude."

"So he left the needle, syringe, stun gun, bottle, and note for us. Let's hope he made a mistake this time. I'll need statements from you and anyone else who was in that room. We'll need comparison prints from all of you to eliminate your prints and hopefully isolate his, though I'm sure he had gloves on."

We settled in to give our statements and have our prints collected, which took another half hour. Finally, we were released to return to the emergency room.

"Doc, we need to find this guy before he hurts someone else," Dirk said.

"I'm glad you feel that way, because I have a plan to turn up the pressure tonight after our shift."

"Count me in."

CHAPTER THIRTEEN

Wednesday, 1:38 p.m.

"Finally, some good news," Teamont said.

"Don't tell me we have an actual lead." Frist replied.

"We do. The stun gun has been traced to a Noah Bonner, who purchased it about three years ago. He registered the warranty with the company."

"What do we know about him?"

"Well, he's probably not our guy. He's seventy-one and lives in Albuquerque at an assisted living facility."

"Definitely not our guy, but maybe he remembers something that can help us. When are we going to talk to him?"

"I was gonna ask the locals to interview him to save us time and money. If he has something valuable, we can fly out there ourselves."

"Didn't Ron Schooner move there a few years ago? He was a solid officer and probably wouldn't mind interviewing the guy."

"Great idea, call him and set it up. Also, the ID number on that bottle of fentanyl indicates that it was checked out at the hospital and given to a patient in the ICU five weeks ago. The records say that it had been used on that patient with the remainder wasted into secure drug disposal."

Frist leaned back in her chair and thought about the implications of the source of the fentanyl. "How did a bottle of fentanyl checked out in the ICU five weeks ago end up being injected into Dr. Waverly's arm by the Avenging Angel? I know we have to get through some privacy laws to see how much was actually used on that patient, but while that is in process, we can at least figure out how the remainder was supposed to have been disposed of. Clearly, it wasn't, so maybe we can find who had access."

"Okay, I'm gonna call Ron, and we still need to get over to Waverly's house to interview the husband." They had spoken to him briefly, but he was too distraught to think straight. They hoped that a second, more thorough interview might yield new information when he was better prepared to talk about it.

The detectives contemplated the case on the car ride to Waverly's house. Teamont broke the silence, as they entered the gated community.

"Apparently, two doctors with no kids can afford to buy a really nice house." The mansions in the spacious, landscaped neighborhood sprawled across private acre lots. Beautifully manicured lawns and gorgeous trees surrounded the houses, providing an additional level of privacy.

"Must be nice to afford vegetation in this desert."

"Yeah, but it's a hell of a lot cheaper to keep the sand and rocks in my yard alive."

They pulled into the circular drive of a traditional stucco home, where Dr. Waverly, freshly showered and dressed in worn sweats, promptly answered the door. The welcome air conditioning refreshed them, as it labored to keep the massive house cool.

"Come in, Detectives."

"Thank you. This is a beautiful house," Frist said.

Dr. Waverly looked around, as if noticing it for the first time. "Yes, it is. Janet chose it and decorated it. Please have a seat over here."

He led them into a large, but comfortable living room, and the Detectives sunk into the plush, gray sofa. Frist took the lead.

"Dr. Waverly, thanks for meeting with us. We know this is a terribly difficult time for you."

"Anything to help catch the killer. Please call me David."

"Okay, David. We wanted to start with your movements this morning starting at about 5:00 a.m."

"Am I a suspect?"

"Technically, everyone in that hospital is a suspect. We can quickly rule you out based on your whereabouts."

"Okay. I had an early morning admission, a patient in congestive heart failure, who came to the sixth floor around five. It took me about forty-five minutes to get her settled into her room. Since I was up, I began my morning rounds, which means that I checked on the nine patients I had to take care of this morning before I turned them over to the daytime physician at eight."

"So during that time, you were on various floors of the hospital."

"Yes. I had to log into the electronic health records at various times, so there should be a trail of where I was."

"Thank you, that's helpful. Now let's turn our attention to your wife. Did Janet have any enemies?"

David teared up. "No one I can think of. She got along well with everyone at the hospital, and our social life is kind of quiet. We lead a pretty simple life. I mean we led a simple life. I guess everything has changed."

"The bottle of fentanyl was identified as one supposedly used in the ICU five weeks ago. Do you have any idea how that bottle ended up in the room today with your wife?"

David appeared genuinely confused. "That doesn't make any sense. Narcotics are tightly controlled in the hospital. Anesthesia uses them every day, of course, but they have procedures to track every bottle. Janet was always complaining about all the time she had to spend to document everything."

"We're looking into that paperwork. Now, tell me about Janet's coworkers."

After they exhausted their questions, they exchanged contact information. David would let them know if he thought of anything new, and they would keep him updated. Back in the car, Teamont slapped his notebook on the dashboard.

"I sure hope Albuquerque leads somewhere, because we have nothing to work with here."

"They should have all the narcotic paperwork ready for review by the time we get back. I'll get started on that," Frist said.

"Enjoy. I'll confirm David's movements in the hospital and then interview everyone who was on shift at that time. Someone had to have seen something. The killer's not invisible."

"The killer's an angel, so maybe he is."

CHAPTER FOURTEEN

Wednesday, 7:30 p.m.

The end of my shift arrived, and I signed the last of my patients' charts. Dirk had been playing with Banshee while he waited for me to walk to the cafeteria. Soon enough, Dirk tore into his ham and cheese submarine sandwich, as Banshee wolfed down a grilled chicken breast, and I laughed inwardly at their uncanny similarities. I stayed with my usual grilled cheese sandwiches and fries, perfectly browned, as always.

"What's your plan, Doc?"

I glanced across the surrounding tables to reassure myself that no one could overhear us. "Well, Dirk, it involves breaking a few rules. Please don't feel like you are obligated to do any of this. I don't want to get you into trouble."

"This may come as a surprise to you, but I've broken a few rules over the years. As long as the goal is noble, I'm in. What do you have in mind?"

"I want to search Chuck Damon's office. He lied to me when he said that the Phantom Files don't exist. I think they do, and Chuck's office would be a convenient place to store them."

"Wouldn't they be on a computer?"

"Probably not. The information is way too sensitive, and any computer can be hacked. My guess is that they have paper files with single copies securely locked somewhere."

"Why the hell would they keep records like that at all?"

"Hospitals are fundamentally risk-averse institutions. No one would want to deal with negative publicity from the revelation of scandalous secrets, but they do want access to their own files, in case an internal problem or lawsuit pops up. Basically, they're afraid to destroy it, because it might be useful some day."

"And you think these files will identify the killer?"

"Not necessarily, but they may tell us who may have a motive to commit these murders. If we can find information in those files on Nielsen and Waverly, we may gain some understanding of why they were targeted. Also, we would know that the killer had to have access either to the files or to the actual experiences they describe. That's got to be a fairly small number of people. We might be able to narrow the pool of suspects to a manageable few."

"So if we find anything, we hand it over to the cops?"

"That's where it gets complicated. We would be breaking the law to get this information. If we tell the cops how we got it, then we put ourselves in jeopardy, and prison is definitely not part of the plan. That said, any information we give them, even obtained illegally, maybe could be used to prosecute the killer, as long as the cops weren't involved at all in the illegal search. So we can't just openly share it with the cops, but of course, we want to help them prevent another murder."

"Then what would we do with the information?"

"Let's worry about that if we actually obtain some information. Right now, we think the files might exist, and we think they might contain information about the victims that might be useful, but we don't know anything, yet."

"So we sneak into HR and break into the office? I'm a little too thick to crawl through any vents."

I laughed at the image of Dirk trying to stuff himself through an air vent. "Actually, we're gonna walk through the front door of HR. It's almost impossible to find anyone left in the administrative offices by 5:01 p.m. The place should be empty. You're gonna settle in at the front desk with a review book and alert me if anyone shows up."

"All I have to do is sit there? How am I supposed to alert you?"

"If anyone comes, tell them you use the quiet office to study at night. Don't worry about the alert. Your softest voice is still loud enough to penetrate the walls."

"How do you plan to access these secure files, if they even exist?"

I held up two small pieces of metal. "Lock picks. I learned how to pick basic locks during overnight calls when I didn't have any patients. A filing cabinet lock should be pretty simple."

"Dirk and Doc Theft Services is officially in business. One thing before we go, though, if we get arrested, I get the bottom bunk."

"Deal, I'm not sure the top bunks are built to withstand your bulk."

Banshee lumbered beside us to take the elevator to the seventh floor. The HR department did not have a formal front door, only an opening off the hallway. The lights were off behind the desk at reception, and Dirk leaned back in the black swivel chair and opened his review book, as Banshee and I entered the main office area. I called into the dark hallway and sensed no one present. I pulled on some latex gloves I had stuffed into my pocket earlier and activated a penlight I had borrowed from the emergency room. Banshee, like a black hole, emitted no sound, as he padded gracefully through the room. I wasn't nearly as quiet but did my best to minimize noise.

Chuck's office door was open, probably for the ease of cleaning at night. The room was a decent size at about twelve feet by fifteen feet. Shelves and a file cabinet lined the back wall, and a moderately sized desk stood alone in front of it. A small table and two chairs stood to the side for more intimate meetings.

I started with the file cabinet on the back wall. It had a simple lock, and as I was reaching for my picks, a better idea occurred to me. I pulled open the shallow top drawer of the desk and found a little silver key among the pens and other detritus common to top desk drawers. Security was important, but convenience more so, apparently.

The key swiftly unlocked the cabinet, and I opened the top drawer that seemed to contain a file for each employee. I found my own, and a quick review showed that it contained the expected, ordinary information of my basic demographics and details of my employment history. The remaining three drawers contained similar files for the rest of the hospital. I looked at Waverly's and Nielsen's files, but learned nothing except that they made a helluva lot more money than emergency room physicians. I gently closed and relocked the file cabinet and started on the desk.

I found nothing of value in the unlocked drawers and turned my attention to the bottom right one, secured by a lock that appeared to be a more complicated addition. I went to work with my picks. Out of practice, I took a few extra minutes to defeat the lock and open the drawer that held a series of files. I removed the first one that turned out to be a case file of an employee suspected of stealing medical supplies. The second file described another employee's allegations of sexual harassment. A total of seventeen files contained information about active HR investigations. None mentioned Nielsen or Waverly.

The last file in the back was unmarked and appeared empty. I almost ignored it, thinking it was an extra file for the next case, but I glimpsed the slim edge of a single sheet of paper. I pulled it out, and under my penlight, I read a list of nine names with seven of them crossed out, including Dr. Waverly and Dr. Nielsen. I did not recognize the other five names, each with a black line through them, but I did recognize one of the remaining two names, a senior physician in the hospital. I did not recognize the final name, Dr. Campos.

I took a picture of the list, returned the file to its original location, and locked the drawer. I double checked that everything looked exactly as I had found it and hurried out of the office with Banshee. We found Dirk so immersed in his review book that he startled when Banshee nudged his leg.

"Damn that dog is quiet. Did you find anything?"

"Yeah, but let's get out of here."

We returned to the cafeteria, where we could sit and talk without attracting attention. I opened my phone and showed the list to Dirk.

"Do you recognize any of the crossed out names besides Waverly and Nielsen?"

Dirk nodded. "I recognize a couple of them, old geezer docs who used to work here. I think they retired or died. What do you make of this list?"

"I think that this is a list of doctors who have files stored elsewhere. HR must keep this list to identify activity involving these doctors. Chuck can probably access them, though."

"Where do you suppose they are?"

"Maybe information this sensitive is secured at a higher level, like in the CEO's office."

"Makes sense. What do you want to do about it?"

I looked around to make sure no one was near. "How do you feel about breaking into another office tonight?"

"I'm in. I assume we go with the same strategy of me at the front door and you checking out the office."

"It worked once. Maybe we'll get lucky again. Let's go."

Once again, we rode the elevator, this time to the eighth floor. The deserted, dimly lit hallways would have given me the creeps, if I hadn't been striding through them with my gigantic friend and my loyal guard dog. As it was, we were probably the apex predators hunting for information that night.

The administrative offices had a glass façade and an unlocked door. Dirk settled behind the desk and opened his book, while Banshee and I melted into the darkness in search of Gentry's office. I went for the corner to find his office exactly where I imagined it would be. The heavy, thick oak door was locked, and it took me several minutes to manage entry.

The tastefully decorated room with no filing cabinets was about twice the size of the one in HR. The shelves showcased awards and pictures of the hospital taken throughout the years. The right side of the massive desk held a single drawer big enough to fit a small refrigerator and featured a sturdy lock. I figured this had to be where the good stuff was kept.

The lock took only a few minutes to open, as my picking skills were slowly coming back to me. I felt like I was opening a treasure chest, as I flung the drawer open, only to find myself confronted with a safe, a clearly sturdy device with a keypad and a fingerprint reader on the front. My heart sank, as I stared at it.

Defeated, I took a picture of the safe before closing the door and made sure everything remained in its original place. I exited the room, locked the door behind me, and heard the front door open.

"Hey, what are you doing in here?"

Banshee tensed at the sound of the new voice, and I motioned for him to remain silent, as we sank back into the shadows. Dirk responded in a disturbingly loud voice.

"Good evening, Officer. How's your night going?"

"Fine. Who are you, and what are you doing in here?"

"I'm studying for my certification exams. I like to come up here at night, because it's so quiet. You won't find any of those fancy suits making noise around here at this hour."

"Ain't that the truth."

"What are you doing up here?"

"Routine sweep of the building. Since the murders of those two doctors, they've increased security and want us to check out the entire building regularly now."

"Oh, well, this area is empty."

"I'll take a quick look around and then get out of your way."

"Take your time."

The Officer entered the main area and swung his flashlight around the room. I hoped he was too unmotivated to turn on the lights, and my pessimistic view of mankind was reconfirmed. He did check to ensure that each office was locked. Banshee and I moved silently ahead of him and carefully stayed outside of the flashlight's beam. By the time he finished his circuit of the room, we had travelled all the way around and were now behind him. He switched off his light and exited.

"Good night, Officer."

"Good night. Be careful up here. That killer could be roaming the hospital."

"Might be better to warn the killer. I'm a pretty big boy and can take care of myself."

"Looks like it. Have a good night."

I heard the officer leave but waited a minute before joining Dirk.

"How did I do, Doc? Was I loud enough?"

"You did great."

"Did you find anything?"

"Only a huge safe I couldn't open."

"Well, that sucks. What now?"

"Let's go home. I need to figure out a way to get into that safe. If the records exist, I bet they're in there."

"Been a fun night out with you, Doc. I got to do a little breaking and entering, lied to a cop, and even got some studying done. We need to do it again."

"Seriously, thanks for your help, Dirk."

We rode the elevator to the ground floor and split up at the garage. Banshee jumped into the front seat and pawed at the window until I opened it. He smiled with his tongue hanging out all the way home.

CHAPTER FIFTEEN

Wednesday, 9:22 p.m.

I took a seat on my back porch and sipped water with a lemon slice and melting ice, as Banshee secured the perimeter of the yard and then collapsed on the cool tile in the shade beside me. I referenced my saved photos and entered the first name from the list into the search bar on my laptop. The physician had worked at my hospital and had died of breast cancer five years before. Searches of the next four names revealed similar histories. All had worked at the hospital and had died within the last five years of apparently natural causes: heart attack, colon cancer, stroke, and heart failure, and the next two on the list had been murdered within the last three days. I searched the last two names on the list, the only two that had not been crossed out.

Nancy Campos had been a pathologist at the hospital for many years and had retired five years before. I found no indication that she had died, but I wasn't able to find out where she was living, either. Based on her work history, she had to be in her seventies.

The last name on the list was Benjamin Haller, a senior cardiologist currently working at the hospital. In his fifties, he had spent his entire career at Tempe Memorial Hospital. As far as I knew, he was in good health.

The list put me in a bit of a quandary. I had obtained it illegally, and therefore it could be used to convict me of breaking and entering. While I was all for being a team player, my desire to do the right thing did not extend to working my way into a jail cell, but I needed to share the information with the authorities. I was pretty sure that Drs. Haller and Campos were at risk of being the next victim, and I had no way to protect them otherwise.

I opened my phone and called Spike, who answered on the first ring.

"Hey, Doc, I assume more poor life decisions have led to this call."

"You've got me figured out. I got a list that I need to share with a police detective, but I can't let him know that it came from me. If I send you a picture of the list with a message, can you get it to him anonymously?"

Spike laughed. "Doc, I'm not sure you understand what I do here. All of my emails are sent anonymously. The best hackers in the world couldn't trace them back to me, so I'm pretty confident that the Phoenix police couldn't either. Send me the image and your message, and I'll get it out tonight. What's the cop's name?"

"Detective Ellen Frist, but I don't have her email."

She scoffed, "Yeah, I can find it. Anything else?"

"Of the nine names on the list, all are doctors and seven of them are deceased. I want to see if you can find anything that links them besides their working at Tempe Memorial Hospital."

"Easy enough. Anything else?"

"Could you please find the last person on the list, Dr. Campos, and give me what you can find on her?"

"All right, Doc. I should have all this by tomorrow morning, and I'll include the bill, or I can just hack into your account and withdraw my fee, if that is easier for you."

"I'll pay. Thank you for your offer of that thoughtful customer service, though. By the way, when do you sleep?"

"Tuesday afternoons and Friday mornings. Later, Doc."

She disconnected, and as always, I felt amazed by her admirable skill and confidence and also terrified of her ability. Maybe I'm naïve, but she seemed to live by a moral code, and there were bigger accounts held by evil people out there for her to borrow from, if she chose. I sent the information to Spike and went to bed pacified by the knowledge that I had done what I could to protect Drs. Campos and Haller, while keeping myself out of trouble.

CHAPTER SIXTEEN

Thursday, 7:03 a.m.

Detective Frist set her coffee on the frayed desk blotter before opening her computer. Her inbox contained the usual spam and bureaucratic BS that wasted a concerning portion of her day, like an update to parking policies for city vehicles, but one subject line caught her attention, "URGENT – NEXT POTENTIAL VICTIMS OF HOSPITAL KILLER." Cynical yet hopeful, she opened it.

"Detective Frist, I need to share this authentic document from Tempe Memorial Hospital. I do not know its significance, but believe it is relevant to your case, as it includes the two recently deceased doctors. The first five doctors are also deceased, and I believe Drs. Campos and Haller may be at risk. I can't say where I found the list or who I am, but I hope it helps. Good luck."

The attached image showed a photo of a list with nine names, seven of them crossed out. She reread the note, printed it, and forwarded the email to her partner. She turned her attention to the sender. The name was a long string of numbers and letters, and the prefix indicated it came from Iceland.

She called the IT department and asked the technician who answered to trace the email. He assured her that he would prioritize it, as her partner walked in and set his bag on the desk. She handed him the printed email and attachment without comment.

Teamont sat on the edge of a worn folding chair they had long ago squeezed into the room and read the email. "I believe the textbooks refer to this as a clue. Unfortunately, I have no freaking idea what it means. Do you think it's real?"

"I think so. It's addressed to me and came via Iceland. Someone went to some trouble to remain anonymous. Regardless of what we might think, we have to follow up on it. With our two victims crossed out on that list, we need to research all nine names to figure out what they have in common."

"You want to start with the five other dead people or the two live ones?"

"Let's both focus on the two live ones. We need to locate and interview them as quickly as possible. We can find someone else to research the other guys. I'll take Campos, and you take Haller."

Three minutes later, Teamont exclaimed, "Done. My guy still works at the hospital. What's taking you so long over there?"

"Campos used to work at the hospital, but it looks like she left about five years ago. I'll have to run her through the database to find her."

Fifteen minutes later, Frist was frustrated. Campos was not in any of the state or national databases normally used to track people. There was no record of her death and no records of social security or Medicare payments. No driver's license information was available. She would have to dig deeper to find Dr. Campos and hope she could keep herself safe in hiding for a little while longer. Frist and Teamont headed back to the hospital to interview Dr. Haller.

. . .

I woke up and checked my phone, unsurprised to see an email from Spike, since last night apparently had not been one of the times she slept. She began the email with her fee and again asked if I preferred the convenience of her deducting it from my account for me. She listed my bank and account number, reminding me of how much access she had. I quickly paid her before I finished the email. I did not want to be on Spike's bad side.

The second paragraph piqued my interest. "All nine of the names are doctors who worked at Tempe Memorial Hospital, and most of them were senior physicians within their departments at the time they left. Nothing stands out except that all nine faced suspensions from the hospital at some point in their careers for unprofessional behavior. No additional information about the allegations exists online. All of them were signed off by a previous CEO."

Hospital suspensions were rare, especially among senior physicians. It was more than a coincidence that all nine had faced suspensions for vague unprofessional behavior. An allegation had to be pretty significant to threaten suspension, and most often, the investigated doctor moved to a new facility rather than remain with a tainted reputation.

The final paragraph was even more interesting. "Haller is currently co-Chief of Cardiology at the hospital, and his record is clean except for a suspension seventeen years ago. His information is attached. Campos went completely off the grid after her retirement five years ago. She spent a lot of money and time erasing her digital footprint and did a pretty good job. I couldn't find her through any traditional databases, but I got lucky. She returned an aquarium pump that was replaced under warranty. The warranty system lists an address in Sedona, Arizona, and a property check reveals that it's owned by a Delaware LLC that was set up around the time she retired. All the utilities are in the business's name, and whoever lives there seems to value privacy. I'm pretty sure that's Dr. Campos. Good luck."

I sat back and marveled at her ability to track someone through a fish pump warranty registration, which made me think that the cops might have a hard time finding Dr. Campos. I doubted that their access included warranty databases. Sedona is only a couple hours north of Phoenix, and I had the day off.

"Banshee, you up for a road trip?"

. . .

"Dr. Haller, I'm Detective Frist and this is Detective Teamont. Could we have a word with you?"

"What's this about?"

"It's better to discuss this in private. Is there someplace quiet we could talk?"

Dr. Haller looked at them inquisitively and motioned for them to follow him into an empty conference room. He sat across from them, folded his hands on the table, and waited for them to begin.

Frist's first impression was that he was curious, but not worried about the interview. In his fifties, his face was dominated by a salt-and-pepper beard, expertly groomed. He squinted his light brown eyes, as if he needed glasses. The unbidden thought that he looked like he belonged in a high-end whiskey commercial more than in a hospital raced across Frist's mind.

"Thank you for giving us a moment of your time. I know you must be very busy."

"I've been busy every day for the last thirty years. What can I help you with?"

"We're investigating the deaths of Dr. Nielsen and Dr. Waverly. Did you know them?"

"I knew them professionally, Waverly better than Nielsen. Cardiology doesn't overlap much with obstetrics, but we've all been around here for years. Any idea who did it?"

"I was going to ask you that question."

Dr. Haller leaned back in his chair. "I figure it has to be someone in the hospital, or at least, someone familiar with them. Once you understand the natural flow of hospitals, it's easy to blend in at any facility, and this took some planning. Hitting two senior doctors within three days doesn't happen by accident."

"You seem to have put some thought into this."

"Damn straight I've been thinking about it. It's all anyone is talking about. Murders in hospitals are rare, and we perceive hospitals as safe spaces for healing, not for violence."

Detective Teamont chimed in. "Dr. Haller, do you recognize the names on this list?" He handed Haller their printed list of names that included Haller's. He quickly scanned it.

"These are all doctors who have worked here, although most have retired. All were senior physicians in their respective departments at the time of retirement. I believe some of them have passed away. Waverly and Nielsen were the only two doctors on this list who were still active, and now they're dead. Wait, do you think this freak killed all of these doctors?"

"We have no evidence of that. We believe that most of those doctors died of natural causes. We are trying to understand the significance of this list."

"Where did it come from?"

"An anonymous source."

"Well, maybe it doesn't have any real significance."

"The sender went to extreme lengths to remain anonymous to send the image. Here is the original. It includes a warning that your life may be in danger."

Haller reviewed the image, and his hands trembled, as he held the paper. The detectives silently allowed the tension to build.

"What the fuck is going on here, Detectives? You barge in here with a mystery list of nine doctors, seven of whom are dead, including two murdered this week in this building, and the only one left alive and still working here is me? Do I have that right?"

Frist leaned toward Dr. Haller. "That's correct. We don't know the source or exact meaning of the list, but you can see why we are concerned for your safety. Until we know more, we have to consider you a potential target for this killer."

"Why me?"

"That's what we're trying to figure out. We need to understand what all of the people on this list have in common, which might point to the killer."

"That's a helluva riddle to solve. So what should I do? I don't like walking around with a target on my back."

"Dr. Haller, just to be clear, you don't have any idea why those nine names, including yours, are on a list?"

"None." He stared at the list and avoided further eye contact with the detectives, who shared this mutual observation with a glance, and Frist moved on.

"We can offer protective custody by putting you in a hotel under a pseudonym until we catch the killer."

"No way. I don't have time for that and God only knows how long that would last."

"Okay, then we recommend added security around you in the hospital. We'll do everything we can to make it as unobtrusive as possible, but there will be more people around you at all times. Do you have an alarm at home?"

"Yes, and a shotgun."

"Keep it handy, but don't go shooting at shadows. We don't want anyone injured. We'll have patrol cruise your street every twenty to thirty minutes to discourage anyone from watching your house. We recommend that you remain vigilant until this is resolved. If you think of anything else that ties together the people on that list, please let us know immediately. Also, please keep quiet about the list. Very few people know about it, and we want to keep it that way."

The detectives retrieved the copy of the list, and Dr. Haller left to resume his patient rounds, after assuring them of his willingness to help in any way he could.

"What do you think?" Frist asked.

"He knows something about that list that he's not sharing with us."

"I agree. Something clicked for him when he saw his name on the original list. Why's he holding back on us?"

"Maybe because he's a bit arrogant and thinks he can solve this without our help. My guess is that he has a secret that he wants to keep badly enough to risk his life."

"I wish him the best, but if he doesn't figure this out soon, he may be the next victim. Come on, let's arrange for coverage on him and track down the rest of that list."

CHAPTER SEVENTEEN

Thursday, 9:20 a.m.

The drive north took about two hours in the light, late morning traffic. Banshee gave up sniffing the gusty wind from his open window twenty minutes into the ride and curled up on the front seat next to me. I closed the windows and welcomed the restful silence. Interstate 17 winds north through a barren landscape with the hills becoming bigger and the valleys deeper the further we travelled.

Sedona is a beautiful little city surrounded by famous red, rocky walls composed of iron oxide. Art, natural beauty, and celebrated heritage enrich the culture of its ten thousand residents and lucky visitors. Sedona is also home to the only McDonalds with green arches, because city officials felt that they matched better with the stunning surroundings than the traditional yellow arches would. Even my macabre goal that day couldn't dampen the peaceful feeling Sedona's natural beauty infused.

Dr. Campos' neighborhood included a collection of modern single-story homes with three or four bedrooms. Every house appeared well cared for, and people strolled along the sidewalks in the dry, mild sunlight.

The address provided by Spike led me to an ivory stucco house where an older woman stooped to plant pink begonias in the front yard under shady eaves. I had pictures of Dr. Campos from her time in the hospital and felt fairly certain that this woman matched the younger version. I needed to see her face to be sure, though. I parked the car and leashed Banshee before opening my door. Dr. Campos looked up at us, and I stopped on the sidewalk, while Banshee sat so as not to frighten her.

"That's a beautiful dog," she commented.

"Thank you. This is Banshee. He's a retired police dog."

"Is he friendly?"

"Extremely friendly, unless he's performing his police duties." I snapped off his leash and gestured toward her, "FRIEND."

Banshee bounded to her, sniffed her hand, and received ear rubs in return. "I keep ruminating about getting a dog, but I don't get out enough to keep one busy. What are you two up to today?"

"I'm looking for Dr. Campos."

Startled, she stopped petting Banshee, stood fully upright, and stared at me with narrowed eyes. "Who are you?"

"I'm AJ Docker, an emergency physician at Tempe Memorial Hospital."

"I assume this has something to do with the murders down there."

"It does."

She considered her options before reaching a decision. "I'm Dr. Campos. Perhaps we should discuss this inside. I could use a glass of lemonade. Would you like some?"

"That sounds nice."

"Is it okay if we leave Banshee in the back yard? I just cleaned the floors."

"Of course."

I led Banshee into the backyard and followed Dr. Campos into the house. The furniture seemed new, and the tastefully decorated house included no visible pictures. The neutral colors warmed in the abundant sunlight that streamed from oversized windows.

"Have a seat on the couch, and I'll get the lemonade."

She brought two tall glasses and set one on a coaster on the table in front of me. She resignedly relaxed in an overstuffed chair across from me, sipped her lemonade, and placed it on another coaster. Her right hand slid from behind her back and revealed a small gun. I sat still, feeling my face drain of color, as I looked down the barrel of a .38 caliber revolver a few feet in front of me, well aware of the tremendous damage it would inflict, if she so chose. Her finger rested inside the trigger guard, ready to exert mild pressure to end my life.

"Sit real still and answer my questions honestly. What are you doing here?"

"I work in the emergency room at Tempe Memorial, and I took care of the two doctors who were murdered there this week. I did some investigating and found a list of doctors that included the names of the two who were killed. Your name was on that list, and you're only one of two still living."

"How did you find me?"

"It wasn't easy. I have a friend who's a computer wiz. She couldn't find you in any normal database. She said you must've had to spend a lot of time and money to erase your digital trail. Finally, she found that you had returned a fish pump for repair. Apparently, the warranty registration still contains your original name, but the address had been updated to this one."

She looked at the aquarium on the side wall and a sad sigh escaped from her lips. "Tell me about the list."

"I'm happy to, but please consider pointing that gun in another direction. I'm not here to hurt you. I'm just trying to keep you and the other doctor alive."

She lowered the gun and placed it next to her leg, still in easy reach, but at least less threatening. I took a deep breath and forcibly relaxed my shoulders.

"The list?"

I slowly reached for my phone, opened it to the picture, and gently slid it across the table. Dr. Campos picked it up and quickly read it before placing my phone on the table and taking another sip of her lemonade.

"Call me Nancy. That list is the reason I made myself so hard to find."

CHAPTER EIGHTEEN

Thursday, 11:57 a.m.

Dr. Haller finished his morning rounds and returned to his office to knock out the documentation before a brief lunch and his afternoon clinical schedule of only seven patients. He completed a few forms but couldn't maintain his focus, as his mind unwillingly wandered back to the list.

He knew every name on that list. He had begun his career thirty-one years before, fresh out of residency. Like most new graduates, he felt like he had worked hard to attain excellent competency, but he soon realized that he wasn't prepared for the real world. The academic world bestowed status and prestige based on title and length of service, but the real world valued hard-earned reputations built over time. His early years had been difficult for him, as he felt perpetually frustrated about the lack of immediate acceptance that he was a brilliant cardiologist. He was indeed a brilliant cardiologist, but he hadn't had a chance to prove it yet.

His frustration boiled over and expressed itself in the form of inappropriate behaviors. If the current sensibilities had applied, he would have been labeled a misogynistic bully, but back in the day, a powerful man's difficult behavior was tolerated. Eventually, his behavior drew the attention of the administration, and he had been ordered to endure counseling to preserve his job. The therapy admittedly softened the rough edges of his worst behavioral tendencies, but his fundamental essence had never changed. He was still a bully, but a more diplomatic one, thanks to therapy.

Dr. Haller possessed enough insight to know why he might be on that list, but he wasn't sure why the others were there with him. Did they commit similar missteps? Was he targeted even now for his mistakes of years before? He didn't scare easily, but the two recent murders had rattled him, especially since he was the only one alive and still working at the hospital.

He picked up his office phone and called the CEO. Gentry might have some answers.

· · ·

"Campos is a ghost," Frist said.

"Really?"

"Yeah. She went off the grid about five years ago and has disappeared from every database I can access. She doesn't get social security or Medicare. I found no banking, no driver's license, and no taxes."

"Maybe she's dead."

"Maybe, but that wouldn't explain why she is scrubbed from the databases. I don't think she's dead; I think she's hiding, which means she might know something important."

"What do you want to do?"

"I asked IT to keep searching for her, while we focus on the rest of the list."

"We need to find her. I bet she has a helluva story."

· · ·

Dr. Campos let Banshee inside through the back door and set a bowl of water in front of him before she settled back into her chair. Banshee curled up on the floor next to her and rested his head on her feet.

"If he's bothering you, Dr. Campos, I can call him over here."

"He's fine, and again, please call me Nancy. My practicing days are long gone. Since you already know and have apparently not disclosed my most valuable secret, my location, I trust you can be discreet with the story I'm about to share."

"You have my word."

"Many years ago, when I was a young and stupid doctor, I made a big mistake. Of course, it started with a young man, a newsman, and we were in love, at least I thought I was in love, but he didn't suffer from such emotions. He used me like he had used other women he had seduced as sources for his stories. At first, I shared idle pillow talk, as he seemed interested in hearing about autopsies I had performed. I believed that sharing the information was harmless, although I knew that I had provided him with a few tidbits for his stories.

"Then, we had a movie star who had overdosed and was scheduled for autopsy the next day. My man convinced me to allow him to attend the autopsy, which of course was against the rules. I trusted that no harm would result from his learning about an autopsy that would be publicized anyway. He hadn't been the first to ask, but he was the first that I allowed in. I left him alone for less than a minute, and during that time, he snapped photos of her nude body. I had no idea that he had done it until the photos showed up in a trashy magazine and then circulated more widely. Of course, the resulting investigation included me, and the hospital took a bad publicity hit. I confronted him and told him I would report him to the police."

She paused to drink her lemonade, and I chose not to interrupt her thoughts.

"He laughed in my face and dared me to report him. He would tell them that I invited him, that it was my idea, and that I had accepted payment for access. I would lose my job, my medical license, and possibly go to jail, not to mention being sued into bankruptcy. This was back when there weren't many women doctors, and we had to be perfect to maintain professional respect. I finally confided in the CEO, prepared to face the consequences and keep my self respect, but he decided to take care of himself."

"He blackmailed you."

"Yes. He drew up a letter describing the transgression I had confessed and asked me sign it. He would keep it, and in return for my letter remaining confidential, I had to kick back twenty percent of my annual salary to him. He made sure that my career advanced and that my salary grew along with his payments."

"What happened to the CEO?"

"He retired about fifteen years ago, and a new CEO took over. I figured I was in the clear, but two weeks into his tenure he called me into his office and showed me the letter. He said that the previous CEO had shared the details of our relationship and that he expected it to continue under the same terms."

"What changed? What made you run and hide your identity?"

"When the latest CEO, Gentry, was hired, he called me in, as well. He wasn't happy with the previous arrangement and demanded fifty percent of my earnings. He said that some other doctors had died and that those money trains had stopped, so I needed to pick up the slack. He added a threat of violence, if I did not comply. Near retirement age, I had compiled a nice nest egg, so I created a new identity and scrubbed all traces of my past from the internet, except I forgot about the fish pump rebate information. I've lived my quiet life here in Sedona. I take care of the yard, go hiking, and have a small circle of friends. Most importantly, I don't have to deal with that hospital any more."

"I'm sorry that happened to you. Do you think the other people on the list were being blackmailed as well?"

"Probably. All of them were senior physicians and had advanced rapidly at the hospital. That was the easiest way for the CEO to maximize his income."

"What I don't get is why someone is killing people on the list. Only four living doctors on the list were left, including you, and now two more are dead. What do you make of that?"

"Maybe those two threatened to stop paying or go public. It ends the gravy train, but it also eliminates the risk of exposure. Plus, the dramatic mechanisms of death will deflect attention away from what is really happening."

"Those guys must have taken home millions over the years. That's a secret worth killing for."

"What's your next step, Doc?"

"I need to get my hands on those files. I'm sure they are locked away in the CEO's office."

"What would you do with them?"

"I will have to see what's in them, but if I find information that identifies the killer, I have to share it with the police."

"Can I ask a favor? If you get a hold of those files, can you destroy mine? I just want to live out my days in peace and quiet."

"I can't make any promises, but I'll do everything in my power to make sure your name remains hidden. I'll even have my friend delete your name from that warranty list. Thank you for sharing your story with me."

"You're welcome. If there's a chance you can get that bastard Gentry in jail, then do what you have to do. He deserves it."

"I agree, but it's complicated. Unless you testify publicly, I don't think the police could get a warrant, let alone a conviction. Your secret is safe with me, but please consider confiding in the police. In the meantime, I'll see if I can get the information another way."

"Thank you, Doc. It does feel good to unload that burden after so many years alone. Take care down there. That man is dangerous."

"Don't worry. Banshee takes good care of me."

I drove back with a snoring Banshee stretched across the back seat. I racked my brain, trying to figure out a way to access that safe.

CHAPTER NINETEEN

Thursday, 3:56 p.m.

Dr. Haller completely ignored the secretary, as he stormed into Gentry's office, where phone in hand, the CEO startled from his leisurely slouch in his tilted desk chair. His secretary followed, apologizing for the intrusion, and Gentry waved her away. He finished his phone call with a promise to call back and motioned for Dr. Haller to take a seat across from him. Fuming, Haller remained standing.

"I wasn't aware we had a meeting on today's schedule, Dr. Haller."

"Cut the shit, Bill. What's going on with these murders, and why am I being dragged into it?"

"What are you talking about?"

"The police just paid me a visit and wanted to know why my name was on a list with Nielsen, Waverly, and six other doctors. I told them I had no idea, which was true at the time, because I never knew who else was on your damn blackmail list. But now I understand, and I want to know why people on that list are dying, especially since I'm the last one alive."

Gentry sat up straight at the mention of the list. "What names were on the list you saw?"

"Me, Nielsen, Waverly, Campos, and a bunch of old timers who have already died."

"How the hell did the police get that list?"

"I wasn't even aware it existed until the cops showed up. Now they think I'm the next target, and I think they're right. Be honest with me. Are you behind these deaths?" His intense stare amused Gentry, as if he could be rattled by a look.

"Why the hell would I be killing people who pay me? In case you haven't figured it out, their deaths leave my bank account a little lighter."

"Sending thoughts and prayers your way during this difficult time, you piece of shit. People are dying, and you're worried about the loss of your parasitic income? I ought to turn your ass in right now."

"You'd be sentencing yourself at the same time, and reporting this to the cops won't stop the killer. That has to be the main objective here, identifying and stopping the killer."

Dr. Haller finally sat on the edge of the chair. "Who has access to that list?"

"I do, and Chuck Damon in HR does, but he doesn't know the significance of it. He knows only to contact me if anything comes up related to people on that list."

"Do you think he would release it?"

"He would have nothing to gain by doing so. He's another one whose record is not as clean as he would like. If I go down, he goes down with me."

"Clearly this avenging angel is on a mission and targeting people with skeletons in their closets, and I have no plans to be the lead story on the news any time soon."

"Someone seems to be cleaning house. We have to stop him. Let me work on Chuck. You get out of here and watch your back until this is over."

Dr. Haller opened the door, but paused before leaving. "If something happens to me, I am blaming you. Remember that!"

The secretary wondered about the drama, as Dr. Haller left as abruptly as he had arrived, and Mr. Gentry quietly closed his office door.

•   •   •

I called Spike on the drive home.

"You in jail yet, Doc?"

"No, but the odds are increasing. Have you made any progress on getting into that safe?"

"Yeah, I identified the model and ran it by some of my friends, who specialize in accessing safes like that. The system is beatable, but you will need a thumbprint of the guy and some specialized equipment."

"What equipment do I need?"

"The kind that's not available in stores. I have a friend who can get into any safe. It's probably best if you bring her along and let her do it. Too many things can go wrong if you try to do it yourself."

"Send her my way. I'm happy to have her on the team."

"She's not gonna be cheap."

"I'm good for it."

"I know, but I'm just giving you a heads up. Probably gonna run you seven to eight thousand."

It was a fair amount of money, given the significant risk. "Give her my number, and I'll set it up. Thanks, Spike."

I knew exactly how to get that thumbprint. "Banshee, I'll need your help on this one."

Banshee thumped his tail against the passenger door.

CHAPTER TWENTY

Thursday, 9:49 p.m.

The killer hummed a senseless tune, as he finished. The clunky device could never win any awards for its engineering efficiency, but it could for its effective innovation, he mused. He had tested it multiple times, and this latest model had exhibited zero failures. Now, all he had to do was get the device in place. That should be easy, as the hospital was usually quiet at night.

He debated for a few more minutes on the exact content of the note. The message was important to keep the investigators' attention focused in the right direction, away from him. Satisfied after several edits, he printed the note and packed everything into his bag before taking off his gloves and collecting the rest of his trash. He would dump it into a hospital waste box scheduled for incineration that night. He drove to the hospital with the senseless tune stuck on repeat bouncing through his mind.

CHAPTER TWENTY-ONE

Friday, 7:12 a.m.

Dr. Haller awoke feeling groggy after a night of disturbed sleep. Dreams of helplessness before certain death haunted him whenever sleep had beckoned. He dressed for work mechanically, and at the last moment, he added his gun to his bag. He had bought the 9 mm Glock years ago and hadn't fired it or even thought about it over the last decade. Although illegal to have it on hospital grounds, that fact was the least of his worries, and he felt safer with it.

On high alert for anyone following him or giving him too much attention, he cautiously drove to the hospital while hyped on enough adrenaline to disguise the weariness he knew would surface later. He noticed nothing out of the ordinary. At the parking garage, he found an open area to leave his car that eliminated the opportunity for someone to sneak up on him. He transferred the gun to the pocket of his white coat and kept his right hand around it, as he rushed into the hospital. Security was prominent in the lobby, but his badge gave him access to the elevators without a search. The trip to his office was unremarkable, and he set his bag on the desk before deciding his next move. He had a few patients on the floor and had to complete the inevitable documentation that had become a priority of modern medicine. He decided to see his patients first, traded the gun in his pocket for a stethoscope, and locked his office on the way out.

His rounds were routine and efficient. Mrs. Sills's congestive heart failure was improving, and he modified her medications accordingly. Hopefully, he would be able to discharge her in the morning. Mr. Jenkins had recovered well after his minor heart attack, and Dr. Haller wrote his discharge orders. Mr. Simpson still retained fluid, and Dr. Haller asked one of his colleagues in nephrology to evaluate the kidney function.

Less than an hour later, he picked up the pile of mail on his end table and moved behind the desk to collapse into his cushioned chair. The pain did not register at first, as multiple needles penetrated his thighs and buttocks, but he did feel the pressure, as medicines were injected too rapidly through each of the needles. He jumped to stand and was about to turn back to look at what was on his seat, when the drugs rushed into his bloodstream.

Fentanyl affected him first by providing a warm flush and a feeling of lightheadedness that caused him to fall back into his chair. Next, the ketamine hit to render him mercifully unaware of his surroundings. Finally, succinylcholine caused fine tremors that progressed to paralysis. All of his muscles went flaccid, including his diaphragm, which controls breathing. It was a combination of drugs commonly used in anesthesia during surgical procedures. The only difference was the doses were much larger than normal, and no one was present to monitor his airway and breathing.

Within four minutes, Dr. Haller was dead without having had a chance to comprehend what his nightmares had foretold. He slumped forward in his chair, where a coworker would find him about an hour later.

.   .   .

"Good morning, Dirk. Ready for whatever comes through the door today?"

"Ready for battle, Doc. You know, I don't want to be the bearer of bad news, but our killer may be due for another strike."

"I was thinking about that on the way in. Hopefully, he's taking an early weekend break."

"That would be nice. Maybe the detectives will catch him before the next hit. By the way, where does our investigation stand?"

I glanced around us to verify that no one could overhear. "A friend gave me a contact who agreed to meet me tonight. She apparently can access that safe, and we can see if those files really exist."

"Your friends seem to have more interesting skill sets than mine do. Do you need me for anything?"

"I could use you as an early warning system, again, if you're available."

"Count me in. Cracking a safe is more exciting than my usual bowling."

"You bowl?"

"My group meets once a month. I have a 220 average."

"Impressive. They have bowling shoes in your size?"

Dirk lifted a massive foot. "I have to special order them. The bowling alley doesn't carry shoes that fit me."

"The circus might. Let's go do no harm."

My first patient, a fifty-nine-year-old woman, had suffered from pain in her hip for several years. I inwardly shuddered, as I read the chart. Chronic pain like that was unlikely to be resolved with an emergency room visit.

"Good morning, Mrs. Nowak. I'm Dr. Docker, and this is my dog, Banshee. I understand you're having some hip pain."

"This damn hip has been hurting me every day for the last eight years."

"I'm sorry to hear that. Is it worse today?"

"No. It's worse when it rains. It's not bad today."

"Okay. Why did you come in here today?"

"Because I'm tired of it hurting."

"Did it start with an injury of some sort?"

"No, it started after a cruise eight years ago. I'm sure there was something wrong with the bed I had on that boat."

I doubted that the bed had injured her, but I forged onward. "Have you seen any other doctors for the pain?"

"I saw an orthopedist. He did an X-ray and said I had arthritis. Gave me some medicine for it."

"Did the medicine help?"

"Never tried it. He prescribed a generic, and I don't take generic medications."

I knew then that it would be another long day in the emergency room.

CHAPTER TWENTY-TWO

Friday, 8:42 a.m.

The Code Blue validated our apprehension. Dreading what we would find, Dirk rushed toward the cardiology offices with the rest of us close behind him. We encountered a controlled scene, as two cardiologists performed CPR on their colleague.

"What do we have?" I asked.

"Found unresponsive, unknown down time. Looks like he was injected with unknown medicines when he sat in his chair."

"Let's intubate him, and Dirk, give him a dose of Narcan, please." The assessment was grim. Pupils were fixed and dilated, and the EKG was in asystole, which meant the odds of any return of circulation were remote. I intubated him, and we continued CPR with multiple doses of medications over fifteen minutes, but ultimately had to call the code.

The staff stood back in defeated silence, as the frantic efforts ceased and solemnity overtook the room.

"Thanks, everybody. There's nothing more we can do. Please stay here until the police arrive. They'll want statements from everyone."

Careful not to touch anything, I looked behind the desk to see the chair with blood-tinged needles sticking out of the padding of the seat. Smears of blood where he had been dragged out of the office and placed on the floor of the wide, empty hallway whispered murder.

Alerted by hospital security, Detectives Frist and Teamont arrived a few minutes later.

"We need to stop meeting like this, Doc," Frist said.

"I was hoping we wouldn't need to speak today."

"What do we have this time?"

"A cardiologist was found unresponsive at his desk. After the staff pulled him into the hallway to begin resuscitation, it looked like he had been stuck in the legs and buttocks with multiple needles sticking out of the seat of his chair. What was injected is unknown."

Frist bent for a closer look at the corpse. "That's Haller, isn't it?"

"Yes. That's Dr. Haller."

"Show me the office real quick."

I pointed into the office, where they cringed at the small bloody spikes poking through the cushion.

"What the actual fuck is going on here?" Teamont asked. "Let's get everyone's names and clear the area. The evidence team can figure out what the hell is going on with that chair. Doc, we'll stop by the emergency room later for your statement. Unfortunately, we know the way."

Dirk and I collected our gear and walked together back to the emergency room.

"Doc, this guy is pissing me off. I may have to have a word with him when we find him."

"Yeah, this is awful."

I filed away thoughts of Dr. Haller to examine later and picked up my next patient's chart that described a forty-four-year-old male with an ankle injury from a fall from a ladder. I felt relieved to focus on something I could fix.

. . .

The evidence team took their time to process the office and document everything with pictures and video. Finally, it was time to take apart the chair. The padding was lifted intact and flipped over to reveal the device, an air bladder with ten tubes sticking out of it, each connected to a needle that penetrated the fabric of the seat. The technicians gasped at the horrifying thought that someone had thoughtfully created such a weapon.

"Whoever did this got in here and pried the seat cushion off the chair, then placed this device under it with all of the needles pointing up. I'm guessing that when the doctor sat down, the needles penetrated into the muscle. As the bag was squashed, the air escaped through the tubes, which pushed drugs into the muscles under pressure. We'll have to test it, of course, but I imagine this could inject fairly large amounts of fluid quickly through all these needles at once. With his weight settled in the chair, it would take him a moment to stand, which would leave more than enough time for the drugs to take effect. Actually, it's a pretty clever design, horrific, but clever."

"Thank you for getting this figured out. Do whatever you need to at the lab to find out what was injected, where all those parts came from, and anything else you can find that can point us in the direction of the killer," Frist said.

"Fantastic. We have a MacGyver Murderer roaming the hospital," Teamont said.

"Don't say that too loud, or the media will run with it. He is a clever son of a bitch with a medical background and some innovative engineering skills."

"And a warped moral code that allows for the killing of doctors. What do you bet the note is in the top drawer of the desk?"

"I'm not gonna take that bet. I'm curious what he has to say this time."

They waited patiently for the evidence team to remove the chair, and then with gloves on, they opened the top drawer. Sitting on top was the letter they anticipated.

The Avenging Angel strikes
Fear in the impure.
The Purification can
Not be stopped.

"I'm pretty underwhelmed," Frist said.

"Agreed. He has nothing new to say."

"I don't think his heart is all in it."

"His heart is certainly in the killings."

"I meant his heart isn't in the writing. I don't get the feeling these notes are meant to do much other than link all the murders together."

"Maybe he's a lot better at killing than writing."

"So we need to look for someone who failed writing in school where small animals were mysteriously found dead but who is smart enough to get a job in a hospital."

"When you put it like that, he sounds like a lunatic."

"Our killer is many scary things, but he's well organized. These killings were planned meticulously and carried out without leaving any clue as to his identity. He didn't have to be anywhere near the crime scenes when two of the murders occurred. The notes link the victims but are full of a bunch of gibberish that lead us nowhere. Three kills in one week with no witnesses inside a crowded hospital is impressive, I have to admit."

"What happens next? Everyone on the list is dead, except for the elusive Dr. Campos. Do you think our guy is done?"

"I hope so. Let's start on the interviews and see if we get lucky. Maybe someone saw something this time."

CHAPTER TWENTY-THREE

Friday, 11:22 a.m.

"Sue, I'll be back in a minute. I'm gonna run upstairs to admin real quick."

"Any news on our killer?"

"No, I just want to update Gentry on what I saw this morning."

Banshee strolled beside me, and I stopped at a vending machine to buy a Diet Coke. I wiped down the surface before opening it and held it only by the bottom third of the can. Mr. Gentry's secretary, enamored with Banshee, laughed at his performance of tricks, while we waited for Gentry to finish a call. His door finally opened, and he invited us in, as Banshee walked across the room on his back legs.

"Come on in. I've heard about that dog knowing a few tricks."

"He's a performer; that's for sure. Would you please hold this for a second, while I fix his vest?"

He held it, while I made meaningless adjustments to Banshee's vest. I took the can back from him, careful to preserve the thumbprint near the top of the can. I settled into a chair across from his desk, but not before scanning the seat cushion.

"I assume you've heard about Dr. Haller," I said.

"Yes. Terrible business. What can you tell me?"

"It looks like the killer designed a device to inject powerful drugs into him as soon as he sat in his chair. No idea what meds were used, but it must have been fast acting, because he apparently didn't call for help."

Gentry leaned back in his swivel chair. "This is unbelievable. This madman is slaughtering doctors right in our hospital."

"It's awful. I wonder how these three particular doctors are connected. I mean, I doubt they were chosen randomly. This guy seems to be on a mission of some sort. Any idea why these doctors were targeted?"

"I have no idea. That's a question for the police to figure out. Why are you so interested?"

"I have been the one to pronounce all three of these people dead, and preventable death bothers me a lot."

"I've read about some of your exploits. You do seem to get overly involved."

"I tend to face challenges rather than run from them."

"Well, I appreciate your willingness to help, but I think this is a matter best left to the police. If there is anything tying these doctors together, I'm sure they will figure it out. In the meantime, focus on your patients and stay safe."

"Of course, I'll leave it to the police, and I'll let you know if I hear anything else."

"Thank you, Dr. Docker. Have a good day."

Banshee performed a back flip for the delighted secretary on our way out. We had the elevator to ourselves on the way down.

"What do you think, good boy? Should we quit and wait for the police to sort everything out?"

Banshee tilted his head and whimpered, as he tried to understand. I rubbed his ears and reassured him.

"You're a good boy, and you know there's no way in hell we are dropping this."

Banshee leaned into my hands.

. . .

Gentry continued to plow through his schedule, distracted the whole time. Now, that doctor, as well as the police, were searching for connections, but everyone on the list was dead, except Campos, and no one had found a trace of her for years. Another problem was that his supplemental income from all of these doctors had now dried up. He made good money as a CEO, but he had become used to the higher income over the years. He would have to modify his lifestyle to account for his loss of income. His secretary's polite knock disrupted his musings. He said nothing, but she poked her head in anyway.

"Mr. Gentry, the police are here to see you."

"Show them in, please."

His headache intensified, as he rose to greet them. Wearing stern expressions, they sat across from him.

"Mr. Gentry, what time did you leave the hospital yesterday?" Teamont opened.

"About six o'clock, my usual time."

"What time did you arrive this morning?"

"Seven-thirty. What is this all about?"

"Just to be clear, are you saying you were not in the hospital from six in the evening yesterday until this morning at seven thirty?"

"I don't think I like your tone."

"Please answer. Were you in the hospital last night?"

"No."

"If we were to check camera footage, we wouldn't find any images of you here in the hospital? If we looked at your phone GPS, it wouldn't show that you were here last night? If we talked to employees, no one would say they saw you here?"

"I don't like what you're suggesting, and I want you to leave."

Neither detective moved. "Mr. Gentry, we are particularly interested in your whereabouts because of an argument you had with Dr. Haller yesterday in this office," Frist explained, expecting that he might be more forthcoming, if she offered a pathway to alleviate his discomfort.

"That wasn't an argument. He was stressed and upset that his colleagues had been murdered. He wanted answers and prevention of further violence, like everyone else does. He wasn't the only concerned doctor to have graced this office over the last week."

"Did any of the other doctors say that they would blame you if something happened to them?"

Gentry paused, as he tried to remember exactly what he had said the day before. "He felt that because I'm in charge of the hospital, I am responsible for everyone's safety, and he was right. I am in charge, and it is my responsibility to assure the safety of everyone in this facility."

Frist abruptly changed the subject to keep him off balance. "What can you tell me about this list?"

Gentry let it rest on his desk, as he read the list. "I've never seen this before."

"Now you've seen it. What stands out to you about that list?"

"I am not familiar with all of the names. None of the doctors who are crossed out, other than Waverly and Nielsen, worked here during my tenure. I knew Dr. Haller, of course. I do not know Dr. Campos. Where did this list come from?"

"It was sent to us anonymously earlier in the week. We have been unable to identify the source."

"You had this list all week and did nothing?"

"We attempted to authenticate it, and we spoke with Dr. Haller to let him know that he might be at risk. We also attempted to locate Dr. Campos but have been unable to do so. We want to know what these three victims have in common with the others on the list."

"Why don't you interview the others?"

"Because they are all deceased, apparently of natural causes. It can't be a coincidence that all three of our victims were on this list. We need to know the connection."

"I'm sorry. Most of those doctors worked here prior to my arrival. Perhaps you should speak to HR about this. They might have more information."

"We plan to."

The detectives tried and failed to gather any new information. Alone with Teamont in the elevator, Frist shared her impression.

"He's holding something back."

"I agree. You think he did it?"

"No, but I think he might have an idea who might have. There's something else going on here."

"He's playing a dangerous game, and the penalty for losing appears to be death. I hope he gets smart and opens up to us before it's too late. Let's go see what HR has to say about the list."

CHAPTER TWENTY-FOUR

Friday, 1:48 p.m.

After I caught up on my patients, I called Spike, as I walked Banshee in the grass outside.

"I got the fingerprint on a Coke can. When is your safe cracker ready to go? I have a feeling things are gonna start disappearing from some files soon."

"She said she can go tonight, if you have a good fingerprint. I'll have her call you to arrange the details."

"What's her name?"

"She's not gonna share her name with you. She goes by Squirrel."

"Squirrel? As in the fuzzy little tree rodent?"

"No. Squirrel as in collector of nuggets of information. Good luck. Don't get caught. You're one of my best customers."

She ended the call, and I returned to work and waited on a call from Squirrel, the master thief.

Dr. Guidry approached me with a worried expression.

"Doc, do you have a minute?"

"Sure. What's up?"

"I got a call from Dr. Connor. He's coming down in a few minutes to talk to me."

"That's a positive development."

"Maybe. He sounded really angry. Do you mind sitting in with me?"

"I'm happy to. We'll add Banshee to the party. He has a knack for convincing people to calm down."

Dr. Connor arrived a few minutes later with his anger apparent on his face. Average sized, he appeared to be in his forties and carried extra pounds on his frame that suggested a preference for beer over exercise. His white coat and badge gave him an air of authoritative confidence, but put him in khakis and a golf shirt, and he would look like a burned out accountant. He approached Dr. Guidry aggressively, stopping uncomfortably close to her to lean into her personal space.

"We need to talk," he said.

Anna stood without a word, forcing him back a step, and led the way to an empty room. Focused on Anna, Dr. Connor didn't notice Banshee and me following until he entered the room.

"Who the hell are you?" he asked.

"AJ Docker, another emergency physician. Nice to meet you, Dr. Connor." I held out my hand, and he reluctantly shook it.

"This is a private conversation. You should leave."

"I asked him to be here."

I closed the door behind me, and we stood awkwardly until Anna broke the silence.

"Thank you for coming by today, Dr. Connor. I wanted to clear the air on some things."

"I was expecting you to apologize for accusing me of being a drug seeker."

"I did not accuse you of anything. I pointed out that your behavior requesting refills of controlled substances, coupled with your history of multiple emergency room visits for pain-related issues over the last year, present a concerning pattern."

"My other visits are not your concern. You have no right to review my records."

"On the contrary, Dr. Connor, it is my duty to review the records of every patient to determine if any of the past history is relevant. In your case, I determined that a pattern was emerging."

Dr. Connor fumed, "I will fucking destroy your career, if you choose to pursue this lie. I will work to have you thrown off the medical staff and have the state Medical Board review your behavior. By the time I am done with you, you won't be able to find a job doing charity work."

To her credit, Anna didn't rise to the rhetoric and responded calmly and quietly. "Dr. Connor, I have concerns that you have a problem with addiction to pain meds. My duty in this situation is crystal clear. For the safety of your patients, I am required to report these concerns to the State Board to allow them to conduct an investigation."

Dr. Connor took a step toward Anna, but Banshee's soft growl caused him to pause. I decided to chime in.

"Dr. Connor, I know this is stressful and difficult to talk about, but it is necessary. You have two options, and how you proceed is up to you. You can self-report to the Board, in which case your admission would be confidential, and your rehab and recovery would not become publicly available information. After you complete the program, your record would be clean. If we report it, the investigation would become public. We would like for you to have the opportunity to self-report and maintain privacy during treatment, but the choice is yours. Please think about your choice over the weekend, and let Dr. Guidry know your decision by Monday. If she doesn't hear from you by then, she will make the report."

Dr. Connor trembled with rage, as he gazed back and forth between us. Finally, his gaze settled on Banshee, and he stormed out of the room without another word and slammed the door behind him.

"That was stressful," Anna said.

"You did the right thing and handled it well."

"What do you think he'll do?"

"I imagine he's gonna pop some of his remaining pills tonight, then hopefully, he gets a good sleep and thinks through his options tomorrow. The self-reporting option is definitely the way to go, if he wants to save his career."

"Thanks for being here. I didn't want to be alone with him acting like that."

"I'm happy to help. Let's see if we can finish this shift with no more drama."

CHAPTER TWENTY-FIVE

Friday, 3:22 p.m.

Chuck Damon fidgeted across from the detectives. Unsurprised by their visit, he immediately registered their unfriendliness.

"You seem nervous, Mr. Damon," Frist pointed out.

"I have two police detectives in my office. That's a bit unusual."

"It has been an unusual week with three murders of prominent doctors on hospital grounds, all of them in a spectacularly nasty way. What can you tell us about the victims?"

"What do you want to know? They're all senior doctors at the hospital."

"Yes, but as head of HR, surely you must have some insight into what these victims may have had in common. I assume that you are privy to information unavailable to others. What connects all of these victims?"

"I don't know. I don't know anything special about those three doctors."

"Can you think of any reason someone might make a list that would include these three names?"

His pounding heart doubled its rate, and he was sure the detectives could hear it across his desk. His nervousness blossomed into fear. "I don't… I don't know anything about a list."

The detectives noted his dilated eyes, the sweat beading on his forehead, and his increased fidgeting and pressed their advantage.

"Are you okay, Mr. Damon? You seem agitated."

"This whole mess is very stressful. I'm in charge of HR for the hospital, and doctors are dead, and now you are treating me like a suspect."

"No one is treating you like a suspect. We've been interviewing several people everyday. Have you ever seen a list that included these three doctors' names?"

"No."

Frist slid a paper across the desk. "Have you ever seen this list?"

Damon nearly fainted. He felt his eyes drawn toward the drawer by his right foot that contained the original and resisted the urge to glance in that direction.

"Where did you get this?"

"Have you seen this list before?"

"No."

"Are you sure? You seemed to recognize it when you first looked at it."

"I don't recognize the list, but I do recognize the names. These are all prominent doctors who used to work here, but have retired, with the three recent victims included. I'm surprised to see all these names together. How are they connected?"

"That's the million dollar question. We've confirmed that eight of the nine names on that list are deceased, and Dr. Campos cannot be located. I'm just wondering who made the list in the first place and who sent it to us the very week that all three of these doctors were killed. That seems like more than a coincidence, doesn't it, Mr. Damon?"

"It does, but I can't help you. I've never seen this list before today."

Damon stuck with his denials, and the detectives gained nothing, other than the certainty that he was lying.

"Thank you for your time, Mr. Damon. If you think of anything new, please call us."

Frist and Teamont left the offices in silence until they were alone in the stairwell.

"Thoughts?" Frist asked.

"He recognized that list, and he's hiding something."

"You think he's our killer?"

"We can't rule him out, but he seems more nervous than I expected our cold killer to be. I'm not sure he could pull it off. Maybe he only sent us the list and is terrified that the killer may target him next."

"I agree. Do we have enough to pull him in for questioning downtown?"

"Not yet, but I think if we keep the pressure on him, he'll crack. Let's do some digging into his background and see if we can place him in the hospital for any of the murders. Maybe he has a decent alibi for at least one of them."

"There's something weird going on in this hospital."

"You mean besides the three murders this week?"

"Yeah, in addition to those."

· · ·

Chuck Damon wasted no time after the detectives left. He bolted his office door, unlocked his drawer, and removed the list from its folder. The original appeared unaltered and had been in that drawer for almost fifteen years, removed only to cross off names or add names, one at a time.

The grim reminder of the hospital's history, as well as its present failings, had outlived its usefulness. He rolled up the paper, placed it in a coffee mug, and lit a corner with a lighter his wife had sent with him along with a scented candle she had chosen for his office. He would light it now to explain the burning scent, in case those detectives came back. He watched the paper burn and swirled the pieces until only black ash remained. He carried the cup to the break room, washed it in the sink, and felt his problems disappear down the drain.

He had no idea who had found it and shared it with the police, but the list was gone now and with it, his connection to this disaster. With the weight lifted from his shoulders, he idly wondered who the killer might be. Someone with access to tightly protected information had reason to target those doctors. In any case, he no longer had anything to do with it.

CHAPTER TWENTY-SIX

Friday, 7:13 p.m.

I headed to the cafeteria content after a shift with enough patients to keep me busy, but not enough to overwhelm me. I felt grateful for the low stress day of patients with straightforward problems I was able to help after Dr. Haller's horrific murder. Not every day in the emergency room is a dumpster fire.

Dirk joined me and Banshee with his tray loaded with a cheeseburger, onion rings, and lasagna. He dove into his food like he had been looking forward to it all day.

"This machine requires fuel to operate at peak efficiency. This is only my first supper. My second will be at about nine tonight. What's the plan?" Dirk fed a piece of his burger to Banshee, which earned eternal loyalty from my dog.

"The safe cracker is supposed to join us any minute now."

"Do you trust her?"

"I don't know her, but I trust the woman who referred her."

We ate in comfortable silence until a woman dressed in scrubs sat at our table without a word and started picking at tomatoes atop a dry salad. Dirk glanced my way, and I shrugged. She reached down for

Banshee to sniff her closed hand and then scratched his ears, as her other hand stabbed at her fresh spinach.

"Hi, I'm Doc, and this is Banshee."

"I know. Who's the tree trunk?"

"That's Dirk."

"Is he part of this?"

"That depends on what you think this is."

She placed her fork on the tray and turned her eyes to mine. "I'm Squirrel. Spike sent me."

I guessed her age to be anywhere from early twenties to late thirties. She wasn't especially tall or short or fat or skinny. Her face was neither pretty nor ugly. Her appearance was most remarkable for being forgettable. She would be difficult to describe and likely walked unnoticed, if she so preferred.

"Nice to meet you, Squirrel," I said.

"Likewise," Dirk said, offering his hand. Her delicate hand barely wrapped around his.

"I understand you need help getting into a Safetell 1283."

"That's correct. Can you do it?"

"I can open it."

"How long will it take?"

"Depends what condition it's in, but probably less than fifteen minutes. Can you get us in the room unobserved? I have an aversion to prison."

"We've been up there before. We can get into the office, and Dirk will act as a lookout at the front of the office. No cameras are in the area, and it should be deserted at this hour."

"Let's get this done. I'm meeting some people later tonight, and I don't want to be late."

"Do you need any equipment?"

She pointed at her backpack. "Everything I need is in there. All I need from you is access and a fingerprint."

"Then let's go."

We cleared our trays into the trash and stepped into the elevator moments later. "Beautiful dog. What's his story?"

"He's a retired police dog, who was injured when he took a bullet for me. Then I got to adopt him."

"Glad he's on our side. Dogs offer excellent defense. I hate having to break into a place with a dog."

We entered the darkened administrative area, and Dirk took his place behind the front desk and opened his review book. "You kids run along, and don't make too much noise. I'll give you a heads up if anyone shows up."

Squirrel and I pulled on latex gloves and approached Gentry's door. It was locked, and I used my picks to open the door within about two minutes.

"Next time, try using a little less force on the tension bar. It'll improve the feel, and you'll be able to open locks like that more quickly."

"Thanks. The safe is over here."

I opened the cabinet door, revealing the safe. Squirrel made sure it was locked. "It's embarrassing when you try to break the code, and it's already unlocked."

She opened her bag and removed a device with LED light bars on both sides and what looked like a camera lens in the middle. She unfolded a tripod and positioned it over the keypad. She slid on a pair of sunglasses and handed an extra pair to me.

"Trust me, you'll want the glasses."

I put them on, and she turned on her device. Brilliant white light shone on the keyboard, and the reflection briefly blinded me even through the sunglasses. Squirrel pushed a button on her machine, and her screen lit up.

"That should take about ten minutes. Let me see the can with the print."

"What the hell is that thing?" I asked, as I handed her the plastic bag containing the coke can.

"It's a laser that maps the keypad down to the last micron. It looks for differences among the keys. That safe requires an eight-digit code, which yields a hundred million possibilities. We know that at least two of the keys aren't used, and the laser will be able to pick those out quickly from the lack of wear and tear. Each button wears down a little bit every time it's pressed, and each one will be worn down a little differently. The first number is always pushed the hardest and will show the most wear. The last number always has a little path worn into it from a finger dragging down after pushing it. Identification of the first and last buttons is easy for the computer."

"What about the six numbers in between?"

"That depends on who is entering the code. People tend to drag their finger in the direction of the next number they are going to push. So if I push the two button and the next number is eight, I will drag my finger down toward the eight. But if the next number is three, I drag my finger to the right. The computer analyzes all the possibilities and comes up with the best options."

"Who thinks up stuff like this?"

"People who like to open things. Here, hold the can for me."

I held the coke can at the base, and she shined a black light around the top of the can, illuminating a complete thumb print.

"This will work perfectly."

She opened a clean bag and placed the can inside, adding a vial which she cracked open before sealing the bag. Fumes filled the bag and surrounded the can.

"That's super glue. The fumes stick to the oil ridges created by the thumb, and should give us a nice print we can lift off of the can. Now we wait."

She sat and leaned back against the desk and stared at the wall, content with her own thoughts. Banshee joined her, and she slowly pet him, as she closed her eyes.

"You're pretty calm about this," I said.

"I've done it a few times, and breaking into an empty office of a hospital executive is not exactly fear-inducing in my line of work."

"How did you get into safe cracking?"

"I've always felt curiosity for how things work, a desire to know hidden secrets, an appetite for danger, and significant disregard for rules and authority figures."

"I can relate to a few of those things."

"Obviously. We're committing a felony."

"Feels like more of a misdemeanor. Did you have a mentor, or do you just watch YouTube videos?"

"You would be shocked how much you can learn from videos, but I did have a partner who taught me a lot."

"Do you still work together?"

"Not for the next three to five years. He got caught leaving a pharmaceutical building after hours. A dog tracked him down and cornered him until the cops arrived."

"That sucks."

"Occupational hazard. Let's get this done. Talk of prison on a job is bad luck."

She removed the can from the bag, and I could see the well formed ridges outlined by the glue. She removed a can and sprayed the area, covering it completely.

"That's latex. Give it a minute to dry, and we will have a perfect mold. We spray it with silicon, and we get a perfect three-dimensional fingerprint that we can place on the sensor."

"I guess fingerprints aren't as secure as I thought."

"Nothing is as secure as you thought. Let's check on the computer."

We put the glasses back on and peered at the screen. It showed eight numbers, five of them green, while the remaining three were yellow.

"The computer is confident on five of the eight numbers. We just need to guess numbers three, four and five, but that is only six possible combinations. Much better than the hundred million combinations we started out with. We try the three, six, and eight in different order until we get the correct code."

She turned off the light, then put the silicone thumbprint over her own thumb.

"Okay, rookie. Give me your best guess on which order to place the three, six, and eight. You have a one in six chance of being correct. It's considered bad luck if you screw up the first time."

"Let's go with six, three, eight."

"Confident. I like that."

She placed her thumb on the scanner, and it clicked green. She punched in the number provided by the computer, adding the six, three, and eight in the appropriate spots. The light turned green, and she pulled the safe open.

"I'm impressed. The safe is yours."

She turned away and started to pack up her gear.

"Don't you want to look inside?"

"Let me know if you find gold bars or bags of diamonds. Otherwise, I'm not interested in a bunch of papers."

The safe contained multiple files with some banded together. The largest group of files rested on the bottom, and I dragged them out first. Each of the nine files was labeled with the name of one of the deceased doctors. I opened Waverly's and skimmed the contents. Five pages detailed damning information. I opened the Haller file next and found six more pages. My initial plan was to photograph the material, but after seeing the contents, I decided to take the originals with me. I placed them in my backpack, and shut the safe.

"Did you find what you wanted?"

"Unfortunately, yes. The mythical Phantom Files actually exist. I'll need some time to review the material, but it looks bad."

"Let's clean up and get out. We've been in here long enough."

We triple checked the area to make sure nothing had been disturbed and that we had left no debris. All was quiet outside the office, and we locked the door on the way out. Dirk was studying hard at the front desk.

"How did it go?" he asked, finally looking up.

"I got what I need. Let's get out of here."

Squirrel shook my hand. "It was a pleasure, Doc. I'm leaving you here. No offense, but I don't want to be seen hanging out with you. Take the elevator, and I'll use the stairs."

She turned on her heel and left us in the lobby.

"Doc, she's kinda strange."

"Yeah, but she knows her stuff. How would you describe her?"

"You know, I have no idea. She kind of blends in with everything, like the color gray."

"Yeah, good description. Let's go. I need to read some files, and you need your second supper."

CHAPTER TWENTY-SEVEN

Friday, 9:12 p.m.

After pulling on my latex gloves from the hospital, I settled into my favorite chair in the living room, kicked my feet up on the ottoman, and opened Dr. Campos' file. Four pages detailed her infraction as well as cases she had apparently mishandled. The next page was a signed confession of her transgressions, and the final page listed neatly handwritten amounts that she had paid over the years. In her case, the blackmail totaled almost three million dollars after the payments had increased with her salary over time. The handwriting changed with the dates, presumably as a new CEO took over the position. I set it aside and opened the second file.

Seven years ago, Dr. Waverly had been caught stealing narcotics from the hospital for her own use. Unnoticed at first, her addiction became more evident as her habit progressed. She was guilty of two crimes, in that she regularly deprived patients in pain of narcotics and altered their records to make it seem like they had actually received them, when in fact, she had stolen them for herself. She had gone through rehab, and the whole thing had been covered up in return for her payments. Another signed confession preceded a note that she had been paying over three hundred thousand dollars a year to keep her failings quiet.

Dr. Haller's file contained allegations of sexual harassment from over a dozen different women, and in one privately reported incident, sexual assault at the hospital.

Dr. Nielsen had bullied staff and had performed unauthorized sterilization on single, pregnant women under his care.

The files of the remaining five physicians contained details of their own mistakes, including theft, fraud, assault, selling prescriptions, falsifying documents, and malpractice.

After reading about these doctors at their worst, I was mentally exhausted and emotionally drained, horrified by their misdeeds and equally appalled by the cover-up and blackmail by those who profited from these crimes. I had no doubt that the murders were connected to these files, but no idea who might be familiar with the transgressions and enraged enough to avenge them. It could be as simple as someone wanting to seek justice for all of the victims, but it came down to access to the files. Whoever the Avenging Angel was, he had to be on a short list of people with access to the information.

I set the documents aside and grabbed a book from the shelf to take my mind off the horrific decisions made by some of my colleagues and finally came up with a plan for one of the files.

CHAPTER TWENTY-EIGHT

Saturday, 7:33 a.m.

Banshee and I got on the road early, and he soon curled up on his seat to nap, while I drove north through light traffic under clear, blue skies. Dr. Campos answered the door dressed in sandy colored, lightweight pants and a loose black t-shirt under a long, black cardigan. She cradled a mug of steaming coffee.

"I didn't expect to see you so soon. Come in. Can I get you anything? Coffee?"

"No, we're fine, thank you. Sorry to bother you so early, but I discovered some more information I wanted to share with you."

"Please have a seat."

I sat on the edge of the offered chair, while Dr. Campos leaned into the back of the couch and patted the cushion next to her. Banshee curled up beside her and gave me his side eye.

"What I'm going to tell you is off the record. When I said that I discovered some information, I really meant that I acquired it through questionably legal means."

She laughed. "It seems like I'm in good company with a fellow criminal. I can assure you that I know how to keep a secret."

"I have no doubt about that. Remember that list I showed you last time? I figured there had to be actual files associated with those names, and I didn't find them in HR, so I guessed that they would be in the CEO's office. I looked around after hours and couldn't find them, but I did find a safe, and last night, I got into it and found nine files, including yours."

I removed her file from my bag and laid it on the table in front of her.

"Did you look at it?"

"I did. I read all of them."

She picked up the file and carefully perused the pages. Tears pooled in her eyes, as she finished the last page and placed the file back on the table. She dabbed her eyes with her sleeve.

"I was young and stupid when I signed that awful confession. He made it clear that I could either sign it, or he would make sure I lost my license and went to jail for my actual mistake. I didn't think I had a choice at the time. I can't believe how much I paid those assholes over the years. What do you plan to do with this?"

"I'm pretty sure that's the original, and I've made no copies. As far as I know, this is the only copy. I want you to have it, so you know that they don't hold power over you anymore."

"For years, I have lived with the threat of that confession getting out. Even now that I'm retired, its exposure would crush me. Thank you, Doc, for this. I can't tell you how much I appreciate it."

She stood, turned on her gas fireplace, opened the file, and fed the papers into it one at a time to watch each document burn. She held up the last page to show me the confession.

"This single piece of paper has terrorized me for decades. That finally ends now."

We watched without speaking, as she rested the paper on its funeral pyre. Its embers finally flickered into harmless gray ash scattered on the floor of the fireplace. I stood as she approached, and she cried into my shoulder, while I hugged her back and said nothing.

"Thank you, Doc."

"You're welcome."

We settled back into our seats, and she stroked Banshee's soft head.

"What do you plan to do with the other files? I assume they contain bullshit salted with some truth, like mine did."

"I haven't decided yet. What do you think I should do?"

She rubbed Banshee's ear. "Tough question. On the one hand, I hate to disparage the reputations of the other doctors, even though they are deceased. On the other hand, I want to expose the bastards who blackmailed us."

"I agree."

"Somehow, these files are related to the recent murders. Exposing the victims may eventually lead to the killer, but you would infuriate hospital administrators for life and antagonize the killer, if you do it."

"That's not a concern. I'll add them to my list of hospital administrators and killers who don't like me."

"Is that a long list?"

"Surprisingly long. I haven't decided yet, but I'm leaning toward public disclosure."

"Whatever you do, I'm sure you will handle it well. Thank you, again, for your help. I feel unburdened for the first time in years."

"You're most welcome. Thank you for sharing your story with me, and don't worry, your secret is safe with me. As far as anyone knows, I've never heard of Dr. Campos nor have I seen her file."

"Thanks, Doc. You're a good man. Safe travels, and watch your back. You may have already caught the killer's attention."

"No worries. I've got Banshee to watch out for me."

She hugged me at the door, as we shared goodbyes, and waved as we drove away. She appeared ten years younger than she had when I first met her.

"We did good today, Banshee."

He thumped his tail and stretched out across the backseat to take another nap.

• • •

Bill Gentry ineffectually smacked the ball as hard as he could before finishing his tennis match without winning a set. Distracted by the alarming events at the hospital, his game was off. He drove home, showered, and dressed before he headed to his office. With luck, the administrative offices would be empty as usual when he came in on Saturdays to get work done without distraction.

To his relief, he strode into his unoccupied suite, settled behind his desk, and habitually checked his emails. He punched in a few terse replies in addition to his categorization and deletion, then turned his attention to the safe.

He had decided last night to destroy the files, as they could no longer benefit him and could implicate him in the coverups and blackmail. The loss of income bothered him most. Nielsen, Waverly, and Haller had been paying him over seven hundred thousand a year.

He pressed his thumb on the scanner, punched in the eight-digit code, and swung the door open on silent hinges. His eyes focused on the contents, but it took him a moment to process that the files were missing.

He frantically removed the remaining contents of the safe, hoping that the files were somehow misplaced beneath something else, but he confirmed that they were gone. He sat back in his chair and closed his eyes to recreate the last time he had been in the safe. He was certain that the files had been there only three days ago and had been since his first day as CEO. Every time he had opened the safe, he saw them resting in the bottom right corner in a neat bundle of nine green folders. Today they were gone.

How the hell had someone gotten into his safe? He was the only one with the code, and it required his fingerprint. More importantly, who had even known enough to break into his safe and steal the files? Chuck

Damon in HR was the only other person who even knew they existed, but he would not benefit from revealing the information. He was part of the cover-up, too.

The mysterious Avenging Angel must have learned about the files somehow and now controlled them. It had to be the killer. No one else could know about them or have a reason to risk taking them. But what was the killer going to do with them? Release them to the public to humiliate him? Release them to the police to implicate him in the murders? Nothing good would come of this. He should have destroyed them years ago.

Bill placed the remaining, comparatively irrelevant contents back into the safe and locked it. He scanned his office in frustration, as if it would offer a clue about what to do about his terrible premonition that he was about to be blackmailed himself.

CHAPTER TWENTY-NINE

Saturday, 11:22 a.m.

"Banshee, how do you feel about a walk?"

Always ready for walks, he barked and swished his tail. Sedona offers some of the most beautiful landscapes in the country, and I looked forward to their solace, as I worked through my next steps. I parked near one of the trailheads and let Banshee out of the car. I carried a leash and allowed him to wander without it.

Perfect weather accompanied us down the trail. I hadn't packed for a long hike, so we would need to keep it short, but the peace and solitude gave me some time to think through possible outcomes of my decisions. The advantage to releasing the files would be to expose crime and possibly lead to the killer's identification, but it would also expose the crimes of the doctors, all of whom were now deceased. Granted, they had all made mistakes, but I felt horrible about damaging their reputations, especially for their families. Protection of the living had to be my first priority.

I idly threw a stick for Banshee, hoping he wouldn't return with a human bone in his mouth like he had in Montana. That alarming discovery had led to my deepest loss, from which a feeble voice locked securely in the back of my mind admitted that I had not recovered. That killer was still imprisoned, while he appealed his death sentence.

I decided that I had no choice but to release the information. The increased likelihood of preventing another murder greatly outweighed the public damage to the doctors' reputations. Now the question was how to release it without ending up in jail myself or in the killer's crosshairs.

I rounded a corner on the trail, and my musings prevented me from immediately noticing two men blocking the path. They casually swung sticks the size of baseball bats. I stopped about ten feet away, probably appearing exactly as I felt, more annoyed than intimidated. Banshee poked his head through a bush he had been snuffling off the trail behind the men, and I signaled to him to remain still and quiet. Banshee became a statue and watched with interest.

"Good morning, gentlemen. Nice day for a walk, isn't it?"

The presumed leader answered. "It is, but you need to pay a toll to go any further."

"Then I'll turn around here."

"You need to pay a toll if you want to go back."

"What's the toll charge?"

"Your wallet and your watch."

"That's an expensive toll to walk on public trails. How about we agree to disagree, and I'll head back, and you gentlemen can get on with your day."

Both men lifted their sticks and advanced two steps. "I said your wallet and your watch. Now."

I held up my hand to give me a moment. "Okay, but SCARE."

Snarling, Banshee leapt at them and snapped his drooling jaws inches away from their arms. Utterly shocked by the sudden appearance of such a demonic apparition, they jumped back and used their sticks to try to distance themselves from him. I called Banshee to my side to sit at alert status.

"Banshee doesn't like tolls. If you come near me again, he will attack and gnaw on your bones. You'll never walk normally again, and if he goes for the groin, you'll never have kids. Make good choices."

Banshee continued to growl with saliva dripping from his teeth, and they backed away. It's amazing how Banshee motivated people to make wiser decisions.

"Good boy. Let's head back to the car."

Banshee frequently checked behind us, as we backtracked. I didn't bother to turn around. When Banshee had my back, I knew I was safe. I called the police who seemed familiar with two brothers known to rob tourists and promised to track them down. I opened the trunk and gave Banshee a drink of water from my cooler before driving home. Hopefully, my bigger problem would work out as well as this incident had.

·   ·   ·

After a shower and lunch, Banshee and I drove to Nielsen's house. From the curb, I admired the stately home with the perfectly manicured yard. A conservatively dressed woman in her sixties answered the door.

"Can I help you?"

"Yes, Mrs. Nielsen? My name is AJ Docker. I'm one of the emergency physicians at Tempe Memorial, and this is Banshee, my service dog. Do you have a moment to talk to us?"

"What's this about?"

"I was on call when your husband was injured, and I took care of him in the emergency room."

"Please, come in. Can I get you anything?"

"That won't be necessary, thank you."

She led us to a bright room with a wall of southern windows overlooking a tree-lined backyard and a small blue pool. She motioned for me to sit on a yellow damask sofa with dark wood trim that turned out to be much more beautiful than comfortable.

"As I mentioned, I was working when we received the Code Blue in radiology. We did everything we could for your husband, and I'm sorry we couldn't do more."

"I'm sure you did everything you could. I've heard that his injuries were not survivable. Tell me, did he suffer?"

"He was not conscious from the time we arrived on scene and wasn't in any pain."

"What kind of a monster would do something like this?'

"I don't think anyone can ever understand such a thing. I was also involved in the care of the other two doctors. Did you know them?"

"I'm sure I've met them at some function over the years, but I didn't know them."

"Do you have any idea why someone would target your husband and the other two doctors? Did they have anything in common or any common enemies at the hospital?"

"Lenny had plenty of enemies at the hospital, but nothing that would rise to the level of murder."

"How about the hospital in general? Your husband was there for a long time. Did he ever mention anything improper or unusual going on at the hospital?"

Her face hardened. "I am not sure what you are suggesting. Are you blaming my husband for his own attack?"

I held up my hand defensively. "I apologize if I seemed to imply that. I don't mean to suggest that your husband brought this on himself in any way. I'm just trying to figure out why three senior doctors were murdered last week. Something must be going on at the hospital."

She stared at me for an awkward moment. "I am sure the police are looking into this. I'm not sure that this is any concern to a junior physician in the emergency room. Now, if you'll excuse me, I have a busy day today."

We stood up simultaneously, as I acknowledged my dismissal. "Again, I'm sorry for your loss."

Banshee and I crossed the street to get back into the car, and I turned to see Mrs. Nielsen staring at us from her window. She seemed to know exactly what her husband had been involved in that could have led to his murder. The question was whether she knew who the killer was. Idling at the next stop sign, I tapped the next address into my GPS.

CHAPTER THIRTY

Saturday, 1:26 p.m.

Dr. Waverly answered the door dressed in a blue t-shirt and scrub bottoms and warily evaluated Banshee.

"What's this about?"

"It's been a few days since your wife's passing. Are you up for talking for a few minutes?"

Dr. Waverly squinted. "Yeah, sorry I didn't recognize you right away, and I wasn't expecting visitors today."

He led us to his living room through the entryway lined with half-filled boxes. "Excuse the mess. I'm trying to get everything packed up. No sense in staying in a five-bedroom house alone."

I settled into the couch, which was not as pretty but infinitely more comfortable than the Nielsen's.

"Thank you for giving me a moment. As you probably remember, I was on the team that responded to attempt her resuscitation. I'm very sorry that we were unable to do more."

"I know that her death isn't your fault. Whoever killed her gave her enough fentanyl to kill three large adults."

"It's still surreal that three doctors were killed last week."

"Yes, horribly, but also elegantly."

"What do you mean?"

"The killer planned and executed these attacks flawlessly. Each one was unique and unexpected and left no clues. The police say they have no idea who did it."

"You sound like you admire the guy."

"No, he's a sick fuck, but I have to admit that he's smart, at least smarter than the cops."

"Any idea how these three murders are related? Anything going on at the hospital that links them?"

"What's your interest in this?"

"I was involved in the resuscitation attempts of all three victims, and that makes it personal for me."

"We all hate to lose patients, even when their deaths are out of our control, but these murders are for the police to handle."

"I'm sure they're doing a thorough job, but in my experience, people who work in hospitals know secrets that the police might never discover. I'm just nosing around to see if I can find a possible link among these doctors."

"Well, good luck with that, but I still think this is better left to the police. Is there anything else you'd like to discuss?

"No, again, I just wanted to apologize that we couldn't do more to save your wife."

"The killer made sure that resuscitation would be impossible."

Banshee and I left him to dismantle his life. In the car, I laid my head on the steering wheel. These discussions were mentally exhausting, and I still had one more to go.

•   •   •

The courier knocked on the door of his ninth stop of the day and waited patiently with at least four more scheduled deliveries before his weekend began. His mind strayed to possible plans for the evening, when the door opened.

"I have a delivery for a Mr. Bill Gentry."

"That's me."

"I'll need you to sign for it."

Bill illegibly signed with his index finger on the computer screen, and the courier left him with a large envelope and receipt. He usually knew when to expect such deliveries on a weekend and didn't recognize the sender, Medtastic with a local PO box for a return address. He tore it open and dumped the contents.

A cheap cell phone clattered on the desktop before a single piece of paper slid over it.

"We need to talk. Keep the phone on, and I will text you directions this evening. Don't trust anyone."

Was an ally, the killer, or a blackmailer reaching out to him? Could it be the police as part of an elaborate sting operation to entrap him? Whatever it was, the note and the phone meant trouble, and he could not afford to ignore them. He ran the note and envelope through his shredder and opened the phone. It had a full charge and no contacts or messages. He confirmed that the ringer was turned on and dropped the phone in his pocket. Fearful of the messages it might bring, he could feel its weight, as he walked out of the office.

·   ·   ·

Determined to complete the last visit, I knocked on the door.

"Good afternoon, Mrs. Haller. I'm AJ Docker, one of the emergency physicians at Tempe Memorial. I took care of your husband. Do you have a moment to talk with me?"

She asked me to sit on an uninviting, green print sofa that was as uncomfortable as it was ugly. She sat in a hardback chair across from me and held my gaze.

"First of all, I want to say how sorry I am for your loss. I wish we could have done more to save him."

"Thank you, but from what the detectives told me, the murderer pumped him full of fentanyl, ketamine, and a paralyzing agent. I can't imagine that anyone could have brought him back."

At least those drugs had been a relatively humane choice. The ketamine and fentanyl would have incapacitated him before he suffocated. Of course, that fact likely would not bring solace to his wife, so I kept it to myself.

"Do they have any suspects?" I asked.

"If they do, they didn't disclose any to me. I told them they need to look at Gentry, but I don't know if they consider him a suspect or not."

"The CEO? Why do you think he had anything to do with the murders?"

"Because he is a horrible man who has been harassing my husband since the first day he arrived. He thinks that the hospital's primary purpose is to provide doctors who will directly fund his retirement accounts. You must be new there, otherwise he would probably be shaking you down, too."

"Surely the detectives would want to follow up on that."

"Oh, they assured me they would look into it, but I'm just a crazy widow, and he's a big important businessman here. Do you really expect them to take it seriously? You're a young man and probably still idealistic. Let me tell you, this world is full of nasty people doing nasty things."

I had already decided not to bring up any knowledge I had of her husband's transgressions that had apparently led to his murder. I had no doubt that Gentry was a scumbag, but her husband had hardly been a beacon of morality. I answered her few questions about our attempts at his resuscitation before disentangling myself from the visit. I politely escaped out the door with Banshee.

"I'm exhausted. Time for some dinner and a movie on the couch. I'm done with people today. How about you?"

Banshee had no idea what I said, but he seemed to agree with me, which was why I liked him more than I did most people.

CHAPTER THIRTY-ONE

Saturday, 7:34 p.m.

The killer meticulously savored each bite of the rare tenderloin he had perfectly grilled and then sent the simple text.

"We need to talk in person. Regular communication devices are compromised. Come to my house at ten tomorrow morning and use the back door. Tell no one."

The killer typed Chuck Damon's address and tapped send.

Bill Gentry flinched, as if an electric current had surged through him, when his phone chimed in his pocket. His dreadful anticipation had weighed on him all day, and he trembled, as he read the message. What did Chuck know that was so important, and what did he mean by compromised communications? Were the police watching him? He sent "OK" and pocketed the phone. Maybe Chuck had stolen the files for himself or knew who had them. In any case, he would have some answers in the morning. He prepared for bed, although he knew that any rest would elude him.

The satisfied killer completed a few final preparations before he slept deeply.

CHAPTER THIRTY-TWO

Sunday, 6:58 a.m.

I settled in front of the computer I usually used shortly before my shift at seven o'clock and looked forward to a calm Sunday morning followed by a chaotic afternoon. Sunday morning was the time for church, family, or recovery from Saturday night's frolicking, which left only the hard core to make their way to the emergency room. My theory was validated, as the doctor completing her night shift checked out only three patients to me.

"Good morning, Doc. Any excitement this morning?" Dirk asked.

"Hopefully not. Been a long week, and I'd like to end it on a high note."

"You know our psycho killer has been doing his thing every other day this week. If he stays on schedule, he's due for another hit today."

"Maybe he believes that Sunday is a day of rest from at least killing."

"I'm not sure this guy is real religious."

"He does refer to himself as an Avenging Angel, which suggests a religious background."

"Well, let's get to work and try to keep the code bag closed today."

I couldn't agree more. Any day the crash cart stayed shut was a good day in the emergency room. Banshee joined me for my first patient of the day, a thirty-seven-year-old man with leg pain, and followed me into the room.

"Good morning, Mr. Duncan. I'm Doc, and this is Banshee, my service dog. What's going on with that leg?"

The man was wearing cargo shorts and a golf shirt and had his right leg propped up on a pillow. He rolled his eyes and blew out a deep breath as he prepared to answer. Before he could say anything, his wife spoke up.

"Go ahead, Superman. Tell him what you did."

With another head shake, he began his story. "I was at my daughter's cheer gym, and they were giving a performance, and all of the parents were invited out on the floor. After the performance, I told my daughter I could still do a back flip on the springy floor. I went to flip, felt a pop in my right ankle, and haven't been able to walk since."

"When did this happen?"

"Last night. I was hoping it would be better in the morning. It's not."

The rest of his history was unremarkable, and I moved closer to examine his leg. I was pretty sure what I would find, and my fears were confirmed, as I examined the back of his leg.

"Mr. Duncan, I'm afraid you've torn your Achilles tendon."

"Don't you need to X-ray it or something to confirm that diagnosis?"

"Usually, yes, but in this case, it is not necessary. If you feel at the back of the ankle, the tendon is not there, and your calf muscle is all bunched up. When it pops, the muscle contracts and the tendon shortens. I'm afraid you're gonna need surgery to repair this."

"Seriously? I am never gonna hear the end of this from my daughter. How long is recovery?"

"The orthopedist will give you all the details, but we're talking months to recover, not weeks. Sit tight, and I'll have someone come down to talk to you about scheduling surgery."

"Thanks, Doc. I'll just sit here and listen to my wife tell me 'I told you so' over and over for the next hour."

I left to call the orthopedist, as Mrs. Duncan explained to him how she knew this was gonna happen.

.   .   .

"Hey Doc, how's your day going?" Sue asked.

"Good so far, but it's early. Have a minute to talk?"

"Sure, let's go to my office."

We settled into chairs, and she peered at me expectantly. I had been dreading this conversation, but I figured Sue had a right to know what was going on.

"I've been doing some digging into these murders and discovered some things this week that are pretty disturbing about the victims. I think I know why they were murdered."

"Have you told the police? I haven't heard anything about any progress on the case."

"That's where it gets a little complicated. The information I found wasn't shared with me voluntarily."

"You mean you stole the information?"

"That's a fair assessment. If that's a problem for you, let's stop right now, so you aren't burdened with the information."

"No, I'm okay with bending a few rules, as long as no one gets hurt, and it brings us closer to the truth."

"I promise I didn't hurt anyone, and I am definitely closing in on the truth. I searched the HR offices and found a list of nine names that included the three doctors recently killed. Five of the remaining doctors had died of natural causes, and the last name on the list was a doctor who retired a few years ago and disappeared. I had some friends with technical skills help me track her down and had a conversation with her."

"What's her name?"

"I promised her I would keep it confidential. She used to work at the hospital, and as a young doctor, she made a mistake that could have cost her her medical license and possibly led to jail time. The CEO at the time agreed to bury it, as long as she paid a significant portion of her salary to the CEO every year. In return, he advanced her career to grow her salary, which increased her payments to himself. This continued for years until she retired, but he wanted her to keep paying. She then decided to change her name and go off the grid."

"That's horrible. Do you think the other doctors on the list were being blackmailed, too?"

"I know they were. Friday night, I had a friend help me access a safe in Gentry's office, and I found the files for all nine doctors. They included documentation of their transgressions and payments over the years."

"You need to give that to the police."

"That's tricky. Because I obtained it illegally, I could get in a lot of trouble, if I admit to what I did. I'm working on a plan to get the information to them, but it would ruin the reputations of those doctors, if their offenses became public, which would be hard on their already grieving families."

"Surely their spouses know what happened. I mean, there would have been an investigation at the time of the offense, and then all that money paid out over the years would be hard not to notice."

"I'm pretty sure they do know. I visited all three spouses yesterday to say I was sorry for their losses. I got the feeling they knew how the murdered doctors were connected, although none specifically told me."

"So does that lead you to the killer?"

"It narrows it down. It has to be someone who knows about the names on the list and is familiar with hospital procedures. The police do have the list and are investigating who might have access to it. I'm hopeful they can figure it out without the files."

"I hope so. These murders need to stop."

"One other thing I want you to know. Dr. Nielsen's initial offense was sterilizing single moms he had operated on. Apparently, he 'accidentally' clipped the fallopian tubes. According to several OR nurses, he did this multiple times over the years before someone called him out on it."

"That's horrible." Realization dawned on her, and she brought her hand to her mouth. "Oh my God, I was expecting to be a single mom when I got pregnant, and he operated on me."

"The files contained no information about any potential victims, but I remembered your story about the surgery for your ectopic pregnancy, and I thought you should know."

Staring at nothing, she sat unnaturally still. "My husband and I wanted to have kids after we got married, but I was never able to get pregnant again. I knew that the risk of infertility was high after an ectopic, but I should have had one good ovary and tube left. I wonder if that son of a bitch cut my other tube."

"I hope not, but however this turns out, I think you're entitled to the information. I'm sorry to be the one to tell you."

"Don't be sorry. I would rather know than wonder why I couldn't get pregnant. Thanks for sharing this. Please give me a few minutes alone."

"Of course. I'm around if you want to talk."

Banshee and I left her to grapple with her loss of what might have been.

CHAPTER THIRTY-THREE

Sunday, 8:57 a.m.

The killer parked at a grocery store a block from Chuck Damon's house. Dressed in a white polo shirt and khaki pants, he donned ordinary black sunglasses and a plain black baseball cap to complete his suburban camouflage. At least he would be difficult to remember and describe, even if anyone were to notice him. He slung his backpack over one shoulder and strolled toward the house.

Damon lived alone in a cozy, single-story home similar to the other houses on the street. As he approached, he placed stickers of a logo of a fictitious courier service on his shirt and hat. He reached into his bag and pulled out an envelope along with a compact Glock 43 he had bought with cash six months before from a gun show, where no record of the transaction existed. He knocked on the door and stepped back with the gun concealed behind the large envelope.

Chuck looked out the window next to the door.

"Delivery for Chuck Damon. I need a signature."

Chuck opened the door, and the killer advanced, thrusting the envelope into Chuck's hand. While he focused on it, the killer thrust the gun into his belly.

"Stay quiet and back up. If you cooperate, you'll be fine."

Chuck, still trying to process the turn of events, backed slowly into the house, and the killer followed and kicked the door closed, locking it behind him. He motioned for Chuck to sit in a worn recliner in the living room, where Chuck finally regained his voice.

"Take what you want and leave."

The killer sat on a stained, blue upholstered couch across from him with the gun pointed at his chest. "This is not a robbery, Chuck."

Realization dawned, and the killer relished Chuck's expression. "You. You're the guy killing our doctors."

"That didn't take you long to figure out, but you have it all wrong. You are the one killing those doctors. You are the Avenging Angel setting things right at the hospital. You are the one who uncovered the injustices and set out to make things right."

"That's crazy. No one will believe that."

"They will when they see your final confession. Chuck, you were on a mission, and now it's complete. You realize that what you did was wrong, so you decided to confess and end your vengeful murder spree. Rather noble of you in my opinion."

"You're insane."

"Probably, but that changes nothing."

The killer advanced and pushed the gun under Chuck's chin. He recoiled from the cold, hard metal and shrank into the chair. The killer pressed the gun more firmly into his neck until Chuck winced.

"Any last words?"

"Fuck you, asshole."

The killer gently depressed the trigger, and the nine millimeter round transected Chuck's airway and base of his tongue before tearing through his brain stem. The pressure wave from the bullet wreaked catastrophic damage, as it exited the back of his head. Brain matter, under the force of the pressure wave, exploded from the exit injury and spattered the back of the wall behind him, though Chuck had died before the bullet left his skull.

"As far as last words go, that wasn't bad, Chuck." He stepped back to admire his work. Chuck's body slumped in his chair, and the bullet track was consistent with a self-inflicted wound. He rested the gun on Chuck's lap and carefully changed his gloves, placing the contaminated ones into a plastic bag before stuffing them into his backpack. He withdrew the note and left it on the table in front of Chuck. Next, he removed a few vials of medicine that were from the same lots as those used in the previous murders. He pressed Chuck's fingers against the bottles, which he placed in a drawer of his nightstand, along with a few syringes and needles.

He didn't expect his guest for another twenty minutes. He unlocked the back door and took a seat at the nearby breakfast table with a view of the street in front of the house and waited.

.   .   .

Bill Gentry drove slowly toward Chuck's house, hoping that Chuck had the files and would be willing to destroy them. He still needed to rely on the police to stop the killer, but with everyone on the list terminated, maybe the killer was done. Regardless, Bill's disappointment simmered over the hard fact that his supplemental income had been similarly terminated. He resolved to polish his resume and send it to headhunters for a new job and a fresh start.

He parked in front of Chuck's neighbor's house for sale two doors down. Disguising his visit to his own Director of Human Resources hadn't occurred to him. He strolled to Chuck's house and up the driveway and opened the gate to the backyard, belatedly concerned that Chuck might own a dog. The vacant, mildly neglected backyard featured a large covered patio to the back door. He knocked gently. Receiving no response, he knocked more firmly. With still no response, he tried the door and found it unlocked. He stuck his head inside.

"Hey, Chuck, it's Bill Gentry. Are you here?"

"I'm in here."

The reply came from somewhere nearby. Gentry closed the door behind him and stepped through the tidy kitchen with a definite bachelor's motif devoid of decorative clutter. He turned toward the living room and felt a presence behind him.

"Don't move. That's a gun against your spine."

Gentry froze, incapacitated with fear. His legs started to tremble, as he waited for the bullet. Instead, the gun nudged him forward.

"Move it. Into the living room."

Gentry concentrated on moving his feet one step at a time and abruptly stopped. His mind couldn't process the horrific sight of Chuck's unnatural position in a recliner with the back of his head splattered on the wall behind him. Bill started to heave, and the killer pushed him forward.

"No need to vomit. He's dead, and he didn't suffer. Now it's time to decide your fate. Sit over there and put the cell phone on the table."

He pointed for Gentry to sit on the couch across from Chuck and positioned himself to stand beside the corpse, forcing Gentry to consider Chuck's violent death, as his killer spoke. Gentry gingerly placed the burner phone on the table between them, and the killer pocketed it.

"Do you know why you're here?"

"Because of the files, but you already have them, so why do you need me?"

The killer paused before answering. "What files are you talking about?"

"The infamous Phantom Files. The files on all of the doctors, detailing their offenses and listing their payments. You broke into my office on Friday and stole them."

The killer paused to consider this new information. He had assumed that such files existed, but he had never bothered to look for them. He had his own list and a general idea of the parts everyone had played. The details hadn't mattered, but concern about someone else's unpredicted involvement had uncomfortably implanted itself in his mind.

"What exactly did each file contain?"

"They summarized embarrassing misdeeds. They included signed confessions from each doctor and lists of their payments over the years. All of the details were in there. That's what we used to make sure they kept paying."

"You piece of shit, you blackmailed them all for years."

"I didn't set up any of it. I inherited it from the previous administration, who gave them second chances. If they had reported them, they would have lost their licenses. Instead, they went on to have successful careers."

"While lining your pockets. Save the excuses. Who else had access to these files?"

"No one. The safe in my office requires my fingerprint and an eight-digit code that I've never shared or even written down."

"Well, according to you, someone got in there and stole the files. Who has them?"

"I don't know."

"Okay, but sadly for you, that means I have no use for you. Do you have any last words?"

"Wait. I have money. Let's work this out."

"I don't want your dirty money, and I don't want to be blackmailed by someone like you for the rest of my life."

"I'm not a bad guy."

The killer wrapped Chuck's dead hand around the handle of the gun and immediately fired two shots into Bill's chest. The first shot entered just right of the sternum, nicking a pulmonary artery and tearing through lung tissue. The second bullet obliterated his left ventricle, causing instantaneous death. Bill slumped sideways, as his blood overtook the previous stains on the sofa.

The killer held the gun in Chuck's hand near his chin and then let it go to stage the positioning consistent with a suicide. Gunpowder residue would cover Chuck's hand, identifying him as the shooter. The killer stood back to review the scene, making sure that the details were correctly staged.

The violent deaths didn't bother the killer. They had been complicit in crimes and had received justice. More importantly, they closed the case for the detectives. Although the files were a disturbing open issue, their contents backed up the apparent murder and suicide.

Satisfied, he tossed his bag over his shoulder and walked out the back door, leaving it unlocked. He exited a gate that led to an alley and checked that it was unoccupied. With his sunglasses and hat back on, he strolled to the parking lot and drove home, unremarkable in every way. He had a little evidence to destroy, and then the matter would be closed, except for the missing files.

CHAPTER THIRTY-FOUR

Sunday, 11:51 a.m.

"How're you feeling?" I asked Sue in the break room after no new patients arrived for nearly an hour.

"I'm okay. I'm still trying to think through how I feel."

"Sorry to dump it on you, but I figured you would want to know."

"I definitely need to know, but I used to think of him as a hero for saving my life and as a tragic victim of senseless violence. Now, I think that he may have been a sociopathic control freak who hurt someone enough for them to think that killing him would make the world a better place. I have to decide what to do with the information, if anything."

I had no words to help her, so I offered only a reassuring smile to comfort her, which seemed to chase away some of the sadness in her eyes.

Dirk stepped up to the small refrigerator and withdrew a takeout hoagie. "I think our hospital killer took a day off, finally. Lately, he's ruined our day well before lunch."

"It's a relief to have had a normal Sunday morning and a chance to eat lunch before the inevitable afternoon rush."

Dirk's overstuffed beef hoagie looked big enough for three people and had Banshee's full attention. Banshee drooled on the floor with his unwavering stare fixed on the sandwich.

"Hey, Doc, do you ever give this poor mutt real food?"

"Sometimes."

Banshee already sat pretty to earn a bite and followed Dirk's commands for roll over, stand, and down.

"You're gonna run out of sandwich before he runs out of tricks," I warned.

"No worries. I brought two."

Dirk removed a second enormous sandwich from his bag.

"Don't spoil him too much. I'm going to see if the lab results on our patient in room two are back. Maybe they're slow up there, too, and they're done already."

"Holler if you need us."

•   •   •

Mrs. Gentry's concern blossomed to alarm after one o'clock. Her husband often went to the office on weekends, but he unfailingly answered texts and calls, even if only briefly. She had tried multiple times. Maybe his phone had failed to charge, or maybe he accidentally turned it off. She finally remembered that their phones were linked and searched "Find My" on her iPhone. She had never used the app and was surprised to see her husband's little round picture on a map of a neighborhood a few miles away. She zoomed in on the exact house and took her car to follow the map.

She parked in front of the home and noticed Bill's car parked a few houses away. She double checked that the map showed that he was in the house she was looking at, not in the one down the street. She rang the bell and knocked with no response. She returned to her car, and feeling ridiculous, she called 911.

"911, what's your location?"

Mrs. Gentry recited the address.

"What's the nature of your emergency?"

"My husband always answers my texts and calls, he hasn't for a few hours today. The phone tracker shows that he's in this house, where no one is answering the door. His car is down the street. I'm concerned that something is wrong, so I'm calling to see if someone could check that he's okay."

The operator rolled her eyes, thinking that his wife hadn't realized that her husband was having an affair. Of course he didn't answer the phone or the door. He was probably shacked up inside with a girl half his age.

"Ma'am, how long has your husband been missing?"

"About four hours."

"We don't get involved with a missing person case until it's been at least twenty-four hours."

"My husband is the CEO at Tempe Memorial Hospital, where those murders occurred last week. That murderer has not been caught, and now my husband is not answering calls. I'm telling you, something is wrong."

"I'm sending officers to that location, ma'am. Please stay on the line."

The dispatcher muted herself on Mrs. Gentry's line and called Detective Frist, who answered immediately.

"This is dispatch. I have a woman on the line who says she's the wife of the CEO at Tempe Memorial Hospital. She can't reach him, but tracked his phone to a house owned by Charles Damon?"

"Add me to the call, please."

Mrs. Gentry explained the situation.

"Please stay in your car. My partner and I will be there in about fifteen minutes."

Frist called Teamont, as she walked out the door. He grabbed his keys and hustled to the address. Minutes later, they met at Mrs. Gentry's car.

"I'm Detective Frist, and this is Detective Teamont. We're handling the investigation at the hospital. Can you please show me the location of his phone on your app?"

Mrs. Gentry handed over her phone.

"And that's his car parked down the street?" Teamont asked.

"Yes. I'm sure."

"Okay, wait here, please."

The detectives ran up the three steps to the front porch and knocked on the door. When they received no response, they banged on the door with their fists and shouted, "Police, please open the door," loud enough for the neighbors to hear. With no response, they split up and circled the house, peeking in each window. They met at the back door. Frist reached out with her hand covered by her shirt and found the door unlocked.

"What do you think? Do we have enough to enter?" Teamont asked.

"We have a phone beacon in that house for the CEO of a hospital who could have been stalked by a murderer, and he's not responding."

"When you put it that way, I think we can declare it an emergency with a life at risk. Let's take a look."

They unholstered their weapons and entered the house. Frist always led the way and covered doors to the right while Teamont followed close behind to cover the left. They proceeded through the kitchen and briefly paused to clear a bathroom and a closet before they reached the living room.

"What a fucking mess. I'm pretty sure that's our CEO and HR Director. After we clear the rest of the house, I'll get a quick video before the evidence team arrives."

"I'll speak with the wife, and you call it in. Ask them to send extra cars to block off the street. This is gonna turn into a circus."

Teamont called dispatch, while Frist steeled herself and marched out the front door to face her fourth death notification of the week and probably her most difficult.

CHAPTER THIRTY-FIVE

Sunday, 2:22 p.m.

"Doc, it sounds like our killer didn't take Sunday off. Guys from EMS say the radio lit up with calls of a double homicide at Chuck Damon's house."

"Who's the other victim?"

"Not confirmed, but rumor has it that Gentry's wife is crying at the scene."

I had always marveled at the efficiency of paramedic gossip. They had enough downtime to monitor the emergency frequencies. When something big was happening, they contacted their friends on scene to get the scoop. The murders may have been officially unconfirmed, but given that the paramedics were reporting it, I tended to believe the story's accuracy.

"Why the hell would Gentry be at Damon's house, where someone killed both of them? Maybe the killer followed Gentry and took advantage of the opportunity," I mused.

"This ruins your theory that Gentry or Damon might be the killer."

"Unless it was a murder-suicide. In any case, we need more information, so let's get back to work."

As I took care of a child with strep throat, I set aside my feelings about the murders. If I had released the files, would they still be alive? I had to save that analysis for later.

. . .

Frist and Teamont had already interviewed Gentry's wife and organized a canvas of the neighborhood. So far, no one had seen anything useful, and Mrs. Gentry genuinely seemed to know nothing helpful.

"What's it look like to you?" Teamont asked, as they scanned the positions of the corpses, as if to beg them for a hint.

"Looks like Damon shot him in the chest and then ate a bullet."

"What do you make of the note?"

They had asked the evidence team to wait to move it until they had a chance to look at everything in place.

This is the final cleansing.
My duty is now complete.
Although noble in nature,
My acts are immoral,
And I must join the fallen
To await my judgment.
The Avenging Angel is no more.

"Kind of dramatic in comparison to the others," Teamont said.

"Our Angel has been a drama queen from day one. What bothers me is the orientation of the letter. Why isn't it facing Damon or Gentry. I would expect him to lay it down in front of him, so he could see it, but it looks like he tossed it onto the table sideways, like an afterthought."

Teamont mimicked walking from Gentry toward Damon and tossing a paper on the table. "Maybe he threw it down as he walked by."

"Maybe, but if a meticulously organized killer was gonna leave a suicide note, wouldn't he carefully position it and maybe even want to look at it right side up?"

"It's hard to predict anyone's behavior, let alone that of a suicidal murderer. How do you figure this went down? Gentry decided to come over and confront Damon at home and gets shot? Then Damon feels guilty, writes the note, and decides to kill himself, too?"

"Damon could have lured him here specifically for the kill. The letter doesn't look like a last minute thing to me. I bet Damon baited him to come over with the intent to kill him and then join him in the afterlife."

"What's the motive? We're pretty sure Damon would have known about the list, but Gentry's name isn't on it."

"Maybe Gentry was gonna rat him out, or maybe Gentry was involved somehow with the guys on the list."

"Too many maybes."

"Let's tear the house apart, check phone and email records, and see what the evidence shows. Maybe we can fill in some blanks. In any case, I think we can safely close the hospital killer case."

"It'll make the Chief happy."

"Along with a bunch of doctors worrying about who's next. Let's get to work."

The search of the house quickly revealed the medicines, needles, and syringes left in Damon's nightstand, but nothing else substantive. At the end of the day, the scene and Damon's confession convinced most people of his responsibility for the killings. Unanswered questions haunted only Frist.

·   ·   ·

Banshee and I arrived at a peacefully silent home, where I made us dinner before lounging on the back porch to watch the evening fade. The story that Damon had shot Gentry and then himself had been all over the news. In theory, it made sense, especially given the additional information from the files. Possibly, Damon had known the details of everyone's failings and wanted to kill everyone involved in the crimes and subsequent cover up, which included Gentry, but I grappled with the problem of the missing medications.

Damon had worked in the hospital, but in an administrative not a clinical role. While he had access to the whole hospital, he would have had significant difficulty with stealing medications, especially narcotics, which were tightly controlled with inventory checked daily. No system was foolproof, but it would take a lot of sophistication and some level of access to steal medicines in the volumes used by the killer. I wasn't sure that Damon could have pulled that off.

On the other hand, Damon had access to everyone's personal information in addition to the list, and he was found dead from a self-inflicted gunshot wound across from Gentry's body. That was pretty damning evidence of a murder-suicide, thoughts of which led me back to the files, still sitting in my home office. They tied Gentry to the murdered doctors, but neither Damon nor his predecessor were mentioned in the files, although Damon probably knew about them.

The question was what to do with the files. I would be in all kinds of trouble for stealing them and holding them back from the police. If I had left them in place, the police would find them when they searched Gentry's office and opened his safe. Of course, that assumes Gentry would not have destroyed the files on his own.

"Banshee, this may come as a surprise, but once again, I find myself in a mess of my own making."

Banshee didn't seem too concerned about my issues, as he tore into a twisted rawhide chew treat at my feet. He did thump his tail a couple times, which I interpreted as emotional support.

Murders generally occur because of love, money, or revenge, the obvious motive in this case, as all of the victims were guilty of various crimes, and the murderer referred to himself as an Avenging Angel. The question was who, besides Damon, could know about all of the crimes and had access to large doses of narcotics.

CHAPTER THIRTY-SIX

Monday, 7:13 a.m.

Ready to face whatever chaos Monday might bring, Banshee and I arrived at work a few minutes early. Patients tended to address problems that they tried to ignore over the weekend on Mondays, so I expected to stay busy.

Around nine, I found Detective Frist waiting for me in my charting area. She gave a hand signal, and Banshee leaped straight up into the air. She gave another, and he rolled over. He waited expectantly for the next command, and she motioned him over for an ear rub, one of his favorite commands.

"He doesn't do that for most people," I said.

"My trainer told me you have to be confident when giving the commands. Dogs can sense your level of commitment. If you don't believe in the command, they won't either. You got a minute to talk?"

"Sure. Let's head to the conference room. It should be empty."

We settled across from each other, and Banshee chose her side of the table again.

"I heard you had a busy Sunday," I said.

"It was hardly a day of rest. It looks like we have things figured out, but we're trying to close a few open questions. I assume you heard that Damon shot Gentry and then killed himself."

"It was the lead story on the news all day."

"I'm going to share a few facts with you that are not public yet. I hope you can help us with an issue, and I assume I can count on your discretion."

"Of course."

"Damon left a note taking responsibility, and we found some extra vials of medicine in his house that matched the ones used by the killer, but we don't know how he obtained the medicine in the first place. We were hoping you could share some ideas on how one might steal such medicines from a hospital."

"Interesting you brought that up, as I was considering that issue last night. Medicines, especially controlled substances, are highly regulated. Here, and at other hospitals where I've worked, they are under lock and key and usually in the Pyxis machine on the floor."

"I'm sorry. What's a Pyxis machine and what floor?"

"The floor is where admitted patients stay overnight. Think of the Pyxis as a vending machine full of medicines and medical supplies, only instead of money, you have to swipe your badge and enter an ID number to get something out. The machine tracks when it is stocked, with exactly how much, and who removes each medication. This system would be difficult to beat, as only certain people have access to it. For instance, even with my badge, I can't access any of the machines on the floor or in the operating areas. Mostly, only nurses access the machines. The only doctors who get in there regularly are anesthesiologists."

"What are the weaknesses in the system?"

"The weakest point is after the medications are out of the machine. Let's say you are a patient who just had knee surgery, and your doctor orders morphine, but only if you are experiencing intense enough pain to ask for it. Now, if you are sleeping through the night with your pain already under control, your nurse could write in your chart that you awoke in pain and requested morphine. The nurse or whoever has access removes a vial of morphine from the Pyxis and documents that it was given to you, but instead, they pocket the vial."

"You make it sound easy."

"It is easy, if the person takes only one or two vials, but the system tracks how much each person takes out. Over time, the system will flag individuals for using too much medicine. You should be able to track the lot numbers back to exactly where they were acquired."

"We did. They all came from the intensive care unit over the last three months."

"Then just look at who signed them out."

"All of the medicines were signed out by different nurses. How do you explain that?"

I leaned back to work through possibilities. It took a moment before I came up with a feasible scenario.

"Our thief is in a position to steal vials of medicine, but knows that they will be tracked to her. So the thief carries the stolen vial, waiting for an opportunity to help a fellow nurse. She switches the vials, using her stolen one and pocketing the one from the other nurse. The patient gets the medicine, and the other nurse doesn't even know about the switch."

"Why are you saying it's a woman?"

"Statistical probability. Most nurses are women, but it could absolutely be a man, of course."

"You make it seem so easy to beat the system."

"Any security system can be beaten when it involves a human performing one of the steps. The reality is that these systems are designed to catch only lazy thieves. Someone smart and motivated can beat any system. Whatever happened here, that's how I would steal controlled substances in a hospital, if I were so inclined."

"Where does that leave us in our search for the source of the medicines?"

"Look for someone who never withdrew any of the medicine vials, the ones who are not on the list from the Pyxis machine. Your medicine thief is probably absent from your current list, but was working at the time those lot numbers were withdrawn from the machine."

"Thanks, Doc. You've given me a lot to consider."

"I'm happy to help. I just can't see Damon having either direct access to the Pyxis or to any opportunity to switch vials. Are there any other anomalies?"

"Every case has anomalies. We assumed he wouldn't use his home or office printer and confirmed that he didn't. We don't know where the notes were printed. Also, the final letter did not have any fingerprints on it."

"Neither did the others," I said.

"True, but we didn't find any gloves in the house. How did Damon get the letter on the table without using gloves or leaving a fingerprint?"

"He could have used a paper towel."

"True, but why be so fastidious with the last letter? Besides, we didn't find a paper towel or anything he could have used. The note says he's the killer of the doctors, Gentry, and himself, so leaving fingerprints wouldn't matter at that point."

"Do you think someone else put it there?"

She held up her hand. "Stop right there. We've got a confession from Damon and no evidence that anyone else was in that room. I'm looking to tie some loose ends, not reopen the case."

"Fine, but you do have legitimate questions. When is the autopsy scheduled?"

"Tomorrow at nine."

"Mind if I show up?'

"For what purpose?"

"I took care of the three doctors and had to explain what happened to each of their heartbroken spouses. That makes this personal for me. If suicide is confirmed, then I'll let it go."

"And if it's not?"

"Then I'll keep trying to figure this out."

Frist considered it for only a moment.

"I'll allow it, but all this stays between us, and you drop it no matter what the autopsy shows."

"Scout's honor," I said, as I raised my right hand.

Frist walked out and shook her head, like she disagreed with her own decision to let me go to the autopsy.

"No way in hell are we dropping this until we have all the answers."

Banshee nuzzled my hand.

CHAPTER THIRTY-SEVEN

Monday, 11:14 a.m.

"Hey, Doc, got a minute?" Dr. Guidry caught up with me between patients.

"Sure. What's up?"

"Dr. Connor's on his way down and wants to talk. Do you mind sitting in with me?"

"Happy to do so, especially given how angry he was last week. We'll bring Banshee, too."

"Thanks. This whole thing is stressing me out."

Dr. Connor rounded the corner holding hands with a tall, slender woman dressed professionally in black slacks and a fitted cashmere sweater.

"This is my wife, Julie. Julie, this is Dr. Guidry and Dr. Docker. I forgot your dog's name."

"This is Banshee."

With introductions out of the way, an awkward silence ensued.

"How about we talk in the conference room?" I suggested.

Everyone filed in and awkwardly chose a seat. The Connors ended up on one side facing Anna and me. Dr. Connor took a deep breath before he spoke.

"First of all, I would like to apologize for my behavior last week. I was out of line and unprofessional. I'm afraid I have not been at my best lately."

"Thank you," Anna replied.

"This whole mess started six months ago, when I dislocated my shoulder. I had previous injuries from my college days, and a simple fall while playing tennis popped it out of joint. I had it reduced in the emergency room, but orthopedics decided I needed surgery to prevent a recurrence. The surgery was unremarkable, but the post op pain was unbearable. Hydrocodone helped at first, but soon even three or four at a time didn't control the pain. My doctor increased my dosage to oxycodone, which helped, but still couldn't eliminate the pain. At some point, my recovery from surgery became all about the pain medication and not the actual pain. My orthopedist tried to get me off the medicine, but I badgered him pretty aggressively. When he wouldn't provide enough, I started making the trips to the emergency room. Over the last couple of months, my whole world has revolved around acquiring more pain meds."

"I'm sorry that happened to you. Addiction can happen more quickly than most people realize," Anna said.

"You don't have to tell me. In addition to the apology, I wanted to thank you for your intervention. You made me realize how bad the problem has progressed. Last night, I filled out the paperwork with the Medical Board to report my problem. I have taken a leave of absence from the hospital and will be heading to an inpatient rehab facility this afternoon. I plan to get clean and get control of my life back."

Mrs. Connor leaned forward as she spoke. "Thank you both for doing the right thing. It's the impetus he needed to change."

"I'm so glad to hear that you are on the path to recovery. I wish you the best of luck," Anna said.

"Thank you. If you'll excuse me, I have time for a last lunch with my wife before I enter rehab. Take care, and thanks, again."

We watched him leave with his wife squeezing his hand and leaning her head on his shoulder.

"You know, Dr. Guidry, it's rare, but sometimes you are rewarded for doing the right thing. Good job standing up to him and congrats on a good outcome."

"Thanks, Doc. I wish every addict's story ended this well."

"Me, too. Let's get back to work. We still have plenty of time to help more people today."

CHAPTER THIRTY-EIGHT

Tuesday, 9:20 a.m.

The brand new autopsy suite at Tempe Memorial Hospital, loaded with sleek, modern technology, couldn't mask its macabre purpose. The sickening scent of formaldehyde permeated the whole pathology department. This unmistakable odor of death would cling to every visitor. Already dressed in scrubs, I had to add only a mask to enter the room. I had left Banshee in the emergency room to save him from having to endure the miasma.

Chuck Damon's body, laid out on the steel table under intensely bright lights, was respectfully covered with a white sheet to preserve his last moments of dignity. Detectives Frist and Teamont entered together, dressed in scrubs borrowed from the hospital. No one wanted their work clothes reeking of death.

The well respected pathologist, Dr. Turner, was a petite woman in her forties who had been with the department since completing her fellowship twelve years earlier. Her discerning eyes scanned the room above her mask.

"Is that everybody?" she asked.

"Yep. Let's get started," Frist said.

"Okay. We have inventoried his clothes and found nothing of interest. The right hand was tested at the scene and showed heavy traces of gunshot residue."

She pulled back the sheet, revealing Chuck Damon's nude corpse. His skin was unnaturally white under the bright lights, and his wound looked horrific. The injury had left his face sunken and misshapen, like a frightening caricature of Chuck. We stood silently, as Dr. Turner began dictating basic information about the case for the record. With that formality completed, she began with her observations of the skin from head to toe, finding no abnormalities other than the gunshot wound in the neck. She brought her magnifying lens in close to study the wound, delicately handling the edges with small tweezers. She turned off the microphone and turned to us.

"This was obviously a contact wound from the powder burns and gas pattern, but there is also evidence of bruising around the wound."

"And the significance of that?" Frist asked.

"It's unusual. The bruising had to occur before death, which means that the gun was jammed forcibly into the soft tissue of the neck. That finding is rare for a suicide. Pushing the gun that hard into the neck would affect the airway and would be extremely uncomfortable."

"Are you saying it's not a suicide?"

"I'm saying it's an anomaly. If you told me a third party held a gun to his neck and pulled the trigger, then this bruising would be a normal finding. It's an unusual finding in suicide, but not unheard of."

"Dr. Turner, will you excuse us for a moment, please?"

"You can use the room next door. I'll catch up on my dictation while you're gone."

Frist gestured for me and Teamont to follow her.

"Doc, what I'm about to say is confidential, and no one outside this room knows it, not even the Chief, and I want to keep it that way."

"I won't even tell Banshee."

"The bruising anomaly comes on top of some other discrepancies related to the note and medications, as we discussed yesterday. This leads us to suspect that Chuck may not be the Avenging Angel and was set up to cover for the killer. Any one of these peculiarities may not be compelling alone, but added together, I think we have a smart killer who made a few minor mistakes."

They both watched me consider the information.

"I'm not surprised. I don't think Chuck could have gotten hold of the meds in the hospital without leaving a trail. For sure, he would have needed help to do it. What are you going to do about it?"

"That's where it gets a little complicated. We want to smoke out the killer, and we want you to help."

"You want to use me as bait?"

"Bait is a little too strong. We want to say that we are still investigating the murders, because a doctor at the hospital has brought up some information that we need to follow up on, like your explanation of the way those controlled substances are tracked. We want to embellish that story to try to get him worried enough to make another mistake and step into the open."

"I may have a better idea, but I'll need an immunity agreement to guarantee that I won't face charges and that my name won't be associated with the files in any report."

Both detectives stared at me under a weighted blanket of awkward silence, as if I were an alien who had spoken to them in a language they had never encountered. Unfortunately, I had seen such expressions from law enforcement before, but I hoped for the best.

"What files?"

"Files that may help you catch the killer, but first, I need you to overlook how I may have acquired them."

Frist sighed. "Okay. As long as you didn't hurt anyone, we will overlook how the files came into your possession."

"No one got hurt. I was the one who found the original list in Chuck's office and sent it to you. I wanted to make sure that the other doctors on the list received some protection. I also tracked down the mysterious Dr. Campos from the list."

"We've spent days trying to track her down. That's obstruction. How the hell did you find her?" Her admirably controlled anger percolated, but I soldiered on.

"I'd prefer not to get into that, but I spoke with her, and she told me about a blackmail ring at the hospital that has been going on for decades. Gentry was the one currently collecting from the doctors, and she guessed that everyone else on the list was being blackmailed like she had been."

"We need to talk to her."

"Not gonna happen. She has a new name and a quiet life where she finally feels safe, and I promised her I would keep her secret. Besides, you don't need her to corroborate the information. I have the files."

She was openly fuming. "Are you aware of the crime of obstruction of justice? Why didn't you give us the evidence as soon as you acquired it? Do I even want to know how you got them?"

"Probably not. I acquired them from Gentry's safe on Friday evening. They document the infractions committed by the murdered doctors and their payouts over the years. I haven't been interfering with your investigation. My intention was to get evidence that I thought you may not be able to reach."

"We need those files." Her desire for the files overpowered her anger, which I interpreted as a good sign.

"You can have them, and they may be what you need to draw the killer out of hiding. You leak that you're reviewing some files that may lead to an alternative suspect before you close the case. Given that and the information that a doctor in the hospital has provided additional information, it might make our killer nervous enough to make a mistake."

"It could work." They both seemed pacified.

"It has to be someone who knows about the list and about Gentry's blackmail and Damon's role in the cover up. He also has to have knowledge of the hospital and have access to the controlled medications. That should be a small pool of potential suspects."

"We still need a motive."

"My bet would be revenge, as all five victims were involved in crimes against patients and the cover up of those crimes. I think our Avenging Angel wanted to take out everyone involved and walk away from it."

"I'll ask Dr. Turner to delay the release of the autopsy results, and I'll put out a statement that we are still investigating new information that has become available from some files held in Mr. Gentry's office and from a doctor who wants to remain anonymous," Frist said.

"In the meantime, we'll dig into all the nurses in the ICU who did not use any of the missing medication vials. We can interview pretty aggressively, which might shake out a description or even an identity of someone who might have taken them," Teamont added.

"The killer had to know Chuck or Gentry to find out about the list, and Chuck would be easier to connect with than the CEO would have been," I added.

"All this will put a target on your back, Doc, but I'll get you the immunity agreement," Frist said.

"I'll be fine. I have Banshee to watch my back."

"All right. Teamont, would you please finish with the autopsy and make sure Dr. Turner waits at least seventy-two hours to post the results? I'm going with Doc to get these files. We'll meet back at the station to review them and then hold a press conference."

CHAPTER THIRTY-NINE

Tuesday, 11:13 a.m.

I set the files on the kitchen counter and pushed them toward Frist. She put on some gloves and took them to the table to read. I left her alone, grabbed a book, and headed to my favorite chair on the back deck. Banshee stayed curled up at her feet, but still kept an eye on me. About a half hour later, she opened the back door and sat beside me on the porch with Banshee following. He stretched out in front of us to nap.

"That is some interesting reading," she said.

"I thought so, too, depressing as hell, though."

"I noticed that there were only eight files. I didn't see one for Dr. Campos."

"Those are all that were in the safe. I never saw a file on her."

"Strange that Gentry would keep files on everyone except her. I wonder what it might've contained."

"I imagine it would be similar to the others, evidence of a mistake made by a young doctor, followed by a decades-long blackmail scheme that overshadowed an otherwise brilliant career, but that's just a guess."

"Maybe the file will show up eventually."

"I doubt it. It wouldn't help you catch the killer anyway."

Frist silently peered at me to let me know that she knew I had lied, but unintimidated, I changed the subject.

"I think the key is the medications. Again, I can't think of any possible way Chuck could have gotten them out of the ICU. We need to look at the nurses with access and the ability to switch vials. Can you get the list of nurses in the ICU and of the ones who supposedly checked out the vials we found?"

"Yes, I already have those."

"Send it to me along with a list of nurses who worked those days but didn't withdraw any of the stolen vials. Give me thirty-six hours to do my thing."

"What exactly is your thing?"

"It's probably best for you to have deniability. If I don't find anything, you can claim ignorance of whatever I have to do. If I do find something, you'll be the first to know."

Anger flashed in her eyes. "If you find anything at all, I want you on the phone to me, immediately, and stay out of trouble. This guy has offed five people already, so I doubt he'll lose sleep over adding you to his kill list." Self-doubt about my further involvement dominated her expression, but I could tell she had already decided to let me help.

"What makes you so sure it's a guy?"

"It's almost always a guy. Women tend not to commit violent crime, and when they do, they're almost always under the influence of a man. Be careful. I'll send the lists and hold the press conference when I get back. Make sure you keep Banshee close."

Banshee lazily lifted his head at the mention of his name. He did make me feel safer.

. . .

"In summary, this remains an open and active investigation. We are waiting on the final results from the autopsies, and in the meantime, we are investigating files recently turned over to us that may explain why these victims were targeted."

Every hand shot up, as questions flew at her.

"Where did these files come from?"

"I cannot disclose their origin, but they were turned over by a concerned employee with inside information about the victims. We are in the process of following up on that information."

"Do you still think Mr. Damon was the killer?" another reporter asked.

"Mr. Damon remains a suspect, but we are still investigating whether he had help or whether he was a victim himself."

Frist artfully deflected further questions without disclosing additional information until the reporters realized that they wouldn't get anything more, and she ended the press conference.

The killer watched, as he struggled to control his alarm and rage. He had done everything perfectly and had expected them to announce that the case was closed. Instead, they spoke of accomplices, new information, and someone at the hospital who stirred up trouble. He had figured that the police would find the files, he reasoned. They led back to Damon, anyway. Why was the investigation ongoing, though?

He was a meticulous man and had carefully thought through every step he had taken over the last two weeks, and in retrospect, he couldn't find any mistakes. He needed more information. He would find out who was helping the police. One more person may need to be eliminated.

·　·　·

I reviewed the list from Frist. All of the vials had been dispensed on the night shift in the ICU, which narrowed the field of suspects significantly. A total of thirteen full-time and twelve part-time nurses regularly worked the ICU nightshifts. I decided to focus on the full-time nurses, since the thefts had occurred on multiple days.

Seven nurses had dispensed the stolen medicines under their own names, and I set them aside. It was possible that the killer had stolen one under his own name, but it seemed more likely that he hadn't, given how meticulously planned the murders seemed to have been. That left six nurses. Of the six, two were male. Given that most killers were male, I focused on them first.

At thirty-seven, Alex Berrea had been an ICU nurse for twelve years. His spotless record contained no issues. He had been on the night schedule for the last four years and often served as a charge nurse. Married with two sons, ages six and eight, he sounded like a family man without time enough to plan and execute the killings.

Philip Connor, twenty-eight and single, had worked at the hospital for only six months. His previous job in an ICU in Kansas City had lasted three years. He had perfect attendance and no disciplinary issues. How likely could it be for him to discover and act on the secrets of the hospital in such a short time?

The files of the other four nurses were similarly unremarkable. Two were married and two were single. All had been on the job at the hospital for at least three years, the longest serving over twelve years. None of them had any obvious issues, but I couldn't expect a personnel file to show that they had tortured small animals as children.

I needed to dig deeper to include their finances, work history, legal troubles, and any dark secrets. I composed an email to Spike to ask her to dig into the backgrounds of these six to look for anything unusual and any connections to Chuck Damon. It was a shot in the dark, but the only idea I had at the moment.

Spike responded quickly. She found no connection between any of the nurses and Chuck Damon, and none of them had any unusual financial activity or legal troubles. They appeared to be six normal nurses living ordinary lives. With nothing better to do, I decided to visit the ICU at night to meet them in person.

CHAPTER FORTY

Tuesday, 3:57 p.m.

As he watched the detectives make their way through the hospital, the killer noted who they interviewed and compared their predictable investigation against his own mental checklist. Their time inside the administrative offices and in Human Resources, where they could learn nothing relevant, concerned him not at all. Likewise, he had predicted their visit to the ICU, as they followed up on the missing medications, an admittedly weak point in his scheme. Still, the detectives would learn nothing in the ICU that could lead back to him.

The detectives' investigation would run its course of dead ends soon, and pressure to close the case would intensify. He felt confident that blame would ultimately fall on Chuck, but the unpredictability of the doctor from the emergency room needled him into irritating distraction. He couldn't know why the detectives kept speaking with him. He had tried to revive three of the victims, but nothing more could be discerned from those failed efforts. The killer considered whether this emergency doctor had been the person referenced in the press conference. He would watch him closely and eliminate him, if necessary.

.   .   .

I didn't have a plan for our visit to the ICU, other than maybe make someone panic enough to reveal another lead, but Banshee and I headed upstairs anyway.

Like much of the hospital, the ICU had been newly renovated and featured the latest amenities. Twelve rooms surrounded a central core, where doctors and nurses could respond to any room within seconds. Large screens displayed data from monitors in each room, and the various beeps and alarms created a symphony meaningful only to the intensive care team.

"Can I help you?" a nurse asked.

"Yes, I'm one of the emergency room doctors, and I wanted to see if I could speak with your charge nurse for a moment."

"Of course. What's with the dog?"

"This is Banshee. Officially, he's a service dog. Unofficially, he's the mascot for the emergency room."

"Looks mean."

"No, he's a sweetheart. Banshee, SMILE."

Banshee stood on his hind legs, smiled for the nurse, and earned a warmer welcome.

"Sit tight. I'll go find Pam."

I watched the ICU team complete their routines. All was calm at the moment, but I knew that could change rapidly. A new patient or an existing patient who coded would set off a flurry of activity. In between episodes of chaos, serenity characterizes the ICU, as the staff methodically dispenses meds, checks vitals, and performs the never-ending task of charting. Some shifts required staff to spend more time with a computer than with patients. Such were the wonders of modern medicine.

"Hello, can I help you?" Her badge identified her as Pam Murray, charge nurse for the ICU. A tight, low ponytail held back her blond hair and accentuated her warm smile. Even her baggy scrubs could not disguise the fact that she kept herself in shape. Like every ICU charge nurse I had ever met, she wielded a penetrating gaze that missed nothing.

"I'm AJ Docker, one of the physicians from the emergency room. Is there somewhere we could talk?"

Banshee and I followed her into a small office cluttered with paperwork despite the modern computer in the middle of it, and sat across from her.

"Thanks for giving me a moment of your time. I know it's always busy up here."

"You got lucky. The chaos monsters are on break right now. How can I help you?"

"I'm sure you're aware of the recent murders in the hospital."

"Yes. It's horrible. All three of the victims rounded on patients here regularly. I can't believe they're gone."

"I'm new here and didn't know them very well, but I did respond to all three resuscitation codes after they were attacked and had to speak to their families. It's been a rough week."

"That's terrible. I saw on the news that crazy guy from Human Resources was behind everything. Glad that scare is over."

"I'm not sure it's over. There are still some open questions, mainly the issue of the medications used by the murderer. I'm sure you're aware that they came from this department, but I don't see how Mr. Damon could have gotten hold of them. What do you think?"

Murray leaned back in her chair. "That sounds like a matter for the police. What exactly is your involvement?"

"I've been unofficially helping the police after I couldn't save any of the three victims. I spent a long time with the detectives, discussing potential ways the medications could have ended up in Damon's hands. I'm wondering if you guys have figured out how it happened."

"Everyone up here has been interviewed by the police and by the administration, and as far as I know, nobody knows what happened. What I do know is that we are all tired of everyone looking at us like we're a bunch of criminals, and I certainly don't appreciate some emergency room doctor coming up here to accuse us of breaking the law and being complicit in the murders."

I held up my hands to slow the rising tide of anger coming at me. "I am not accusing anyone of anything. I'm just seeking some answers about what happened to three of my patients, and the police thought I might be able to help. Obviously, it was a mistake to come up here. I'm sorry I wasted your time. I'll let you get back to work."

I stood and left her seething, thankful that nothing hit me in the back as I walked out. Relieved, as the elevator doors closed on the awkwardness I had left behind, I looked down at Banshee's apparent unawareness of it.

"Well, boy, do you think we stirred up enough trouble?"

Banshee tilted his head. I was confused, too.

•   •   •

"What did that doctor want?" one of the nurses asked Pam.

"He asked about the missing medicines."

"Why the hell is an emergency room doctor asking about the missing meds?"

"He said he treated all three of the victims and is working with the police."

"I hope you told him to go to hell."

"I let my resting bitch face do the talking. He scampered out pretty quickly. I doubt he'll be back."

It didn't take long for the entire staff of the intensive care unit to hear about the visit from the emergency room doctor. With tensions high over the fact that the medicinal weaponry had come from the ICU, general consensus was that he should stay on the ground floor where he belonged. Eventually, conversation turned to other matters, but anger at the invasive emergency room doctor simmered under the surface.

During the last hour of her shift, Pam broke away to make the phone call.

"Good morning, did I wake you?"

"No, I'm up. How was your shift?"

"Good, except we had a visit from an emergency room doctor who asked about the missing meds. He said he's working with the police."

"Okay, I'll handle it. Just keep your head down and stay quiet. This will blow over soon."

"Okay. I gotta get back to work. Love ya."

"Love you, too."

CHAPTER FORTY-ONE

Wednesday, 10:44 a.m.

During a lull in the action, I wandered to the break room, where Sue sipped a cup of steaming black coffee and Dirk voraciously went after a roast beef sandwich. Banshee ran to Dirk and sat at attention.

"Let me guess. Second breakfast?" I asked.

"Nah, that was an hour ago. This is midmorning snack."

"Any new information on Gentry and Damon?" Sue asked.

"Not really. Everything is tied up nice and neat except for the stolen medications. There is no way Chuck could have gotten them out of the ICU. I stopped by last night and talked to the charge nurse."

"How did that go," Dirk asked between bites.

"Let's just say if I die an untimely death, your first suspect should be the ICU charge nurse."

"They do tend to be fanatical about protecting their territory. May be safer tangling with the murderer than with the night crew."

"I'll keep that in mind. In the meantime, I have some patients to see. Banshee, you joining me, or are you on Team Dirk?"

Banshee looked from me to Dirk and his sandwich, then settled on the floor next to Dirk. His traitorous decision was rewarded with a piece of Dirk's sandwich. I left the two of them and returned to work.

My next patient was a fourteen-year-old boy with a limp that had progressed over the last month. I gathered my stethoscope from the counter and headed to room nine.

"Good morning. I'm Dr. Docker, but call me Doc. Are you Timmy?"

The shy boy nodded and looked away.

"Do you know this lady, or was she just sitting in the room when you got here?"

Timmy cracked a smile. "That's my mom."

"Do you mind if I ask her some questions?"

"That's fine." He turned his attention back to his iPad. History revealed progressive pain and limp in the right hip with no known injury. Ibuprofen had seemed to help at first, but didn't seem to make a difference lately. They had seen their pediatrician, who thought it was a simple strain, but mom was concerned about how much worse the pain had become and brought him to the emergency room.

Physical exam was remarkable for limited range of motion in the right hip. When I asked him to walk, he had a distinctive limp which favored the right hip with his foot turned outward.

"Timmy, I think we need to get an X-ray of that hip. It's just a camera that can take a picture of your bones. Does that sound like a plan to you?"

"It's okay with me."

A short while later, I had the X-rays on the screen that showed displacement of the femoral head and widening of the physis of the joint. I brought my computer into the room to show the patient and his mom.

"It looks like we have an answer for that limp. The X-rays show evidence of a slipped capital femoral epiphysis, which is a fancy way of saying the head of the femur is slipping off the body of the femur at the growth plate. No one knows what causes it, but it is most common in boys undergoing a rapid growth spurt."

"Is it serious?" the mom asked.

"It's more serious than a strain, but it can be fixed. I am going to refer you to an orthopedic surgeon who specializes in this condition. He'll probably want an MRI, and he can go over the treatment options with you after he reviews the scans. He may recommend therapy, or it may require surgical correction. The important thing in the meantime is to take it easy."

Timmy had one of the rare cases seen in the emergency room in which we can make a diagnosis and formulate a treatment plan for a chronic condition. Timmy likely needed surgery, but long term, he would probably fully recover.

Happy to have been able to give them a solid plan and reassure them, my enthusiasm for my job faded with my next patient, a chronic alcoholic vomiting blood.

CHAPTER FORTY-TWO

Wednesday, 6:58 p.m.

I filled a large tumbler with chilled water and grabbed a bully stick for Banshee from the pantry before we lounged on the back porch, where the sunset blanketed the distant hills. Banshee rested on the cool concrete and gnawed on his chew treat.

I hadn't expected an instant revelation from my trip to the ICU, but I had certainly hoped for more than the nothing I got. Word of my visit would have spread quickly, and if it created any consternation among the guilty, I had seen no sign of it. I watched some birds lazily ride the remaining thermals in the dusky sky and then closed my eyes, as I thought through the case. Maybe I had dismissed a relevant observation along the way.

Banshee's low growl, probably due to a squirrel's invasion of his perimeter, disturbed my musings. As I opened my eyes, Banshee jumped to his feet, barked ferociously, and then whimpered and collapsed with his whole body trembling.

I followed the source of the two wires attached to his chest to find a man holding a taser in one hand and a handgun in the other. The average-sized man wearing jeans, tennis shoes, and a blue sweatshirt looked nondescript, except for the hockey mask covering his face and the gloved hands clutching the guns.

"If you want the dog to live, lock him in the house." Although muffled by the mask, his icy calm voice made his intentions clear.

I gently scooped Banshee, still limp from the electrical assault, into my arms and kissed his head. "You'll be all right, good boy. You just need a little time for the muscles to recover." His eyes tried to focus on me but had a hard time maintaining a line of vision. I placed him on the kitchen floor, pulled the taser barbs from his chest, stroked his head, and returned to the patio to face the armed man. At least Banshee was safe.

"What do you want?" I asked.

"Answers, but we're going somewhere more private, where I'll have more time. Get on the floor face down."

I slowly lowered myself to the ground.

"Cross your legs and hands behind your back."

"I assume this is about the murders at the hospital."

"Aren't you the fucking genius. You should have stayed out of it."

"How do you think this plan will turn out? They're gonna know Damon wasn't the guy."

"Why, only because of your disappearance? No one will find your body, and I won't leave a trail."

I could hear Banshee stirring on the other side of the door. "You went to obsessive extremes for vengeance for those doctors' mistakes and the resulting coverup."

"Vengeance? Shut the fuck up and cross your legs with your hands behind your back."

I moved slowly and saw Banshee snarling through the glass door. He barked viciously, as the man grabbed my wrist and looped a zip tie around it with his knee planted in my back and the gun in my spine. He pulled my right wrist into place, looping another zip tie around it, before pulling both of them uncomfortably tight. He stood up and surveyed his work, as I tested the unbreakable bonds.

Banshee, fully awake and barking ferociously, pawed frantically at the scratched glass. The man reached under my arm and pulled me up, keeping the gun on me, and stood behind me with the gun in my back.

"We're gonna quietly walk to my car, or I'll shoot you and your dog here. Understand?"

"I understand. Let me say goodbye to Banshee and calm him down, so he doesn't hurt himself."

Miraculously, he let me turn toward Banshee, fully recovered and ready for battle. We locked eyes.

"GUN."

Banshee launched from his powerful back legs and his eighty pounds impacted the glass door with startling force. The pane bowed outward and shattered, as Banshee's head burst through the door, led by his teeth, thirsty for the man who had hurt him. His paws pressed firmly against the concrete patio, and he used his momentum to hurl himself into our attacker and lock his powerful jaws around the arm with the gun. It flew from his hand, and Banshee released his grip, as his momentum carried him off the porch. The man instantly spun away from me and ran for the corner of the house. Banshee recovered his balance on the grass and turned to pursue him, but I noticed heavy bleeding on his side.

"Banshee, GUARD ME."

Banshee reflexively took a position in front of me with his eyes focused on the retreating attacker. Bloody saliva dripped from his mouth, and his constant growl emanated from his whole body. Although I doubted he even considered returning, the hospital killer was fortunate that Banshee had been cut by the broken glass and held back. Otherwise, Banshee may have torn his arm off.

"Relax, boy. You did good."

His growling lessened but didn't dissipate completely. I located a sizable piece of glass by the shattered door and crouched down to grab it. I sawed through the zip tie with minimal damage to my wrists and turned my attention back to Banshee, still dripping blood from his matted side. I gently parted his fur to find a four-inch cut that penetrated into the muscle. I grabbed a towel from the kitchen and held pressure on the wound, as I took my phone from my pocket.

"Detective Frist," she answered.

"It's Doc from the emergency room. The killer just visited my house. He had planned to kidnap and interrogate me before disappearing my corpse."

"Are you okay?"

"I'm fine, but Banshee has a cut on his side that needs stitched. You'll want to send an evidence team out here. He left his gun and some blood for you."

"I'm on my way. Don't touch anything and don't leave."

I reclined in my lawn chair with Banshee on my lap, as I held pressure on his wound. "I'm proud of you, boy. I wasn't sure you were gonna jump through that door, but I should have known a little glass wouldn't stop you. You're such a good boy."

Banshee licked my chin, as if he could never have become our attacker's demonic nightmare. I surveyed the damage. The window had been tempered glass, which had limited the number of shards, but it had completely shattered. The handgun remained in place on the porch, surrounded by twinkling bits of glass and spattered blood.

Sirens pealed in the distance until the officers first to arrive shouted warnings and approached with weapons drawn. I held tightly onto Banshee where they could see my hands until they holstered their guns. They stretched yellow tape around a wide perimeter, as we waited for the detectives. Frist and Teamont gingerly stepped around the opposite side of the house where our attacker had not run from Banshee.

"You sure you're okay, Doc? There's a lot of blood."

"None of it's mine. Banshee has a decent cut on his flank, but nothing serious. The rest of the blood over there is from the bad guy. Banshee chomped his right arm that held his gun."

"I'm sorry we put you in this position. I never expected him to come after you like this. I had envisioned a more subtle approach."

"It's okay. I volunteered to be bait. I guess my visit to the ICU last night triggered more than I realized."

"Give me a quick rundown of what happened, and then go get Banshee taken care of. You can meet me at the station later for a more detailed debrief."

I ran through everything as best as I could remember, while Frist recorded the conversation.

"Did you recognize him?"

"No, he's an average-sized guy, and I was distracted by the gun and his tasing Banshee. His voice was muffled by the mask, and I didn't recognize it."

"We've got the gun and some blood, so we'll get him. Go take care of Banshee now, and I'll see you soon."

I tightly wrapped Banshee's wound with gauze from an officer's first aid kit before putting him in the car to go get stitches. During the entire ride, Banshee's eyes searched for the man who had attacked us. He would be unable to surprise Banshee again.

CHAPTER FORTY-THREE

Wednesday, 9:22 p.m.

Dirk saw us arrive at the ambulance entrance to the emergency room, luckily nearly empty of patients, and rushed to Banshee. By now, his blood had soaked through the gauze in an expanding red stain.

"What the hell happened?"

"He's fine. He cut himself by jumping through a glass door."

"Why'd he do that? A squirrel outside pissed him off?"

"Actually, he was disarming the man who tried to kidnap and kill me."

"Seriously?"

"Yep. Help me get the supplies, and I'll tell you about it while we fix him up."

"Here? Why not go to a vet?"

"They charge too much. It's a simple cut that I can fix myself."

I took an open room at the back, and Banshee leapt onto the bed as directed. After we gathered the supplies, I cut the gauze off and took a closer look at the wound under the bright lights. Thankfully, it wasn't as deep as I had originally thought with only a few of the deeper muscle fibers nicked.

"Sit still, boy. You're about to get a bad haircut."

Familiar with clippers, Banshee didn't mind the trim. I shaved all the fur, leaving an inch bare on each side of the straight cut. Dirk rubbed Banshee's ears and told him about European soccer standings in his sweetest, soothing voice. Banshee did seem to relax, lulled to boredom by the conversation, its own form of anesthesia.

I washed the wound with two liters of saline under high pressure to make sure all the dirt, debris, and glass cleared. Anything left inside would likely cause infection.

Numbing it with lidocaine made me a little nervous, because the medicine stung when injected. I mixed it with bicarbonate to lessen the burn and told Dirk to be careful.

"Banshee, STILL," I said, and I slowly injected the medicine. Banshee lifted his head to watch me. "Relax, Banshee. It's okay." He didn't take his eyes off me the entire time, but he did remain still throughout the multiple injections.

"He's better behaved than most adults are," Dirk said.

"People could learn a lot from watching how dogs behave under stress."

Banshee laid his head back down on the table. The hard part was over, and I had a clean and fully numbed wound to repair.

"Staples or stitches, Doc?"

"Staples. He's not gonna care about the cosmetic outcome, and I know he's not gonna sit still for ten days to recover. Staples will be much stronger."

"Plus, his scar will look badass."

"That it will, Dirk. He'll be a regular tough guy on the street."

I pulled the edges of the gash together and clicked the stapler, inserting a staple that held the edges in place. Banshee startled a little at the noise, but calmed with reassurance. It took less than a minute to place the remaining twelve staples and seal the wound. I wiped away the blood, and he sported a clean patch of hide with thirteen shiny staples.

"Thirteen is an unlucky number, Doc."

"Maybe, but he was lucky to get only one cut charging through that glass. I think the unlucky one will be the guy who did this, if Banshee catches up to him."

"So what happened exactly?"

I told the story, as we cleaned up the room. Banshee hopped off the bed and spun in circles, as he tried to get his nose closer to the wound to investigate. Fortunately, he couldn't reach it and would not be able to bite the staples out.

"Damn, Doc. Good thing Banshee was around."

"I'm always lucky to have Banshee. Thanks for your help, Dirk. We need to get going. I have a date with the police to share the details."

"Be careful out there."

"Don't worry. I will be."

. . .

The modern police station hosted me in a comfortable conference room rather than in an interrogation room. Teamont and Frist settled into chairs across from me, their energy high, as they closed in on their target.

"How's Banshee?" Frist asked.

"He's fine. He has a few staples in him for about ten days, and then he'll sport a badass scar. He was a perfect patient and didn't complain at all."

"Glad to hear he's doing well. That was quite the heroic effort he made to save you."

"He was committed, that's for sure. Tell me you identified the guy."

"Not yet. The gun didn't have any prints. We are tracing the serial number and will check ballistics, but that will take a little time. Unless he registered it in his name or used it in a previous crime, it won't lead anywhere, anyway."

"What about the blood?"

"We have a clean sample and will enter the DNA into the database, but unless he's already in there, it can't identify him. It takes about forty-eight hours to get results. It will help convict him, if we can identify him at anytime in the future."

"Did the neighbors see anything?"

"We haven't found anyone who saw the perpetrator or his vehicle."

"Unbelievable. I get one weed in my yard, and two hours later, I have an email from the property managers saying someone complained about my yard, but a killer walks around with two guns, a hockey mask, and a bloody arm, and no one sees anything."

"They'll probably send you a notice for the blood stains on your driveway."

"I assume you are watching emergency rooms and clinics for any male with a wounded right forearm that looks like a dog bite."

"We have circulated a description of the wound to local health officials. Have you remembered anything else?"

"No. He was so calm and confident. The thought of taking on me and Banshee should intimidate most people, and he surprised us and neutralized Banshee without a fuss. His plan should have worked and almost did. He couldn't have predicted that Banshee could get through that window. I wasn't even sure he could do it."

"Why do you think the killer took such a bold step? He risked being seen and getting caught. Plus, he confirmed that he set Damon up to take the blame."

"Clearly, my snooping around made him nervous, and he wanted to take me somewhere to force me to give information. I'm not sure what I might know that concerns him that much, and he seemed to confirm that I didn't know who he is. My visit to the ICU must have triggered him, so the medicines must be a point of concern for him, which means that someone up there can identify him."

"Anything else you can remember? A smell? An accent? A tattoo? Any unique phrases or body movements?"

"No, he was just an ordinary guy, and the mask really muffled his speech."

"We need to keep you safe and want to set you up in a hotel under an alias."

"I don't think he'll be back, and if he does return, we'll be ready. Banshee will be on alert, and I have a shotgun by my bed. I don't think he can surprise us a second time."

"The offer stands, if you change your mind. Maybe let the neighborhood know to be on the alert for strangers in the area. Otherwise, call us if you think of anything else."

As Banshee and I left the station, I ruminated on the incident to try to shake out additional details that could be important. I shook my head in frustration, as I drove and took solace in the fact that the killer probably had to contend with a very sore arm.

CHAPTER FORTY-FOUR

Wednesday, 9:37 p.m.

Dr. David Waverly sat on the tile floor in his shower and gingerly sprayed the ragged wound on his forearm. Dog bites are nasty, and this one was deep. Given the high risk of infection, he sprayed the water under high pressure into the wound to clean out the bacteria and debris. The burning pain centered him and focused his fury at the turn of events.

The plan should have worked. He had meticulously set up Chuck Damon as the killer, but somehow the police had seen through his ruse. He had no idea what mistake he had made, as he had planned each step down to the finest detail. He did know that the emergency doctor had somehow inserted himself into the otherwise predictable investigation, and a few minutes alone with him would have clarified his position and allowed him to control the damage. He still deemed the risk he took to capture him worth the chance to cover his tracks. He had anticipated every possibility, except that wild beast's blasting through the glass to rip his arm off. Anger spurred him to clean more vigorously and spark a new level of pain.

His plan had taken root over a year ago during an innocent dinner with Chuck Damon, who had been a fellow freshman at Notre Dame and had lived in a minuscule dorm room across the hall. Although they hadn't been close friends, the shared experience had formed a lifelong bond. They hadn't seen each other since graduation, but after Chuck joined the staff at the hospital, they had reconnected.

Chuck had brought up the list, cautiously at first, and asked if David was aware of any scandals going on behind the scenes at the hospital. David had heard rumors, but every work environment harbored gossip. Chuck confirmed that the secrets were more than mere stories. Several doctors had made mistakes that had been hushed up, and the current administration blackmailed them.

David had known about his wife's transgression, but he had hoped that Chuck spoke only about other doctors. Chuck confirmed his fear that Janet was indeed on the list. The news stunned and infuriated him that the administration of the respected hospital would sink to such a low level and that his wife had betrayed him through her lie of omission. She had never even hinted at the blackmail, but in hindsight, he realized that he should have guessed. They were both high earners with no children and still failed to accumulate wealth. Janet had handled the finances, but that situation was about to change.

David reviewed their bank accounts and discovered multiple payments listed twice, one for a legitimate payment and the other a fake payment, designed to set aside money for the blackmail.

He didn't confront his wife, and his resentment festered until they became distant, which could have been attributed to the long hours and stress of their work lives, but David knew the truth. She had lied about their finances and had stolen money from him.

His affair with Pam in the ICU had been inevitable, as his alienation from his wife deepened. He and Pam had been discreet, as the hospital's social network would have viewed their relationship negatively.

At some point, he decided that his wife had to go, not through an expensive divorce, but permanently. She would have taken half of their net worth, and she had already stolen a large portion of it. If she died, he would keep everything plus the four million dollars in life insurance. She had to be held accountable for her betrayal. She deserved it.

Well aware that he would be the primary suspect of her murder, he pondered the problem for months before a solution came to him. He would be a suspect only if she were the sole victim.

The conversation with Chuck had repeatedly haunted his dreams. Three doctors guilty of significant infractions had never faced consequences. In fact, their careers had been advanced to benefit the CEO, who was worse than the doctors, and Chuck helped cover it all up.

His plan took shape with a series of dramatic murders in the hospital that would lead to Chuck and the list. Pam helped him acquire the medications he needed. The MRI murder and the killing through the seat cushion carried a high likelihood of success, but ultimately, it didn't matter whether they survived. Only his wife had to die, so even though he put himself at much greater risk, he handled that one in person to make sure.

Each step of his plan had gone perfectly, and when Gentry and Chuck ended up dead in an apparent murder and suicide, the whole ordeal should have been over. He would get the house, the insurance money, and the chance to settle down with Pam after a socially acceptable period of grief. The sins of the hospital would have been the lasting legacy, as everyone forgot about the shitty people he had beneficially eliminated.

Somehow, his choreography had fallen apart, and he felt certain that the emergency doctor had something to do with it. He still wanted that information, but it was a moot point after this failure. The police had his gun and his DNA. The untraceable gun didn't concern him, but the blood scared him. He was sure that his DNA was not on file, but if anyone ever checked for any reason at all, he would be confirmed as the one responsible for the attempted abduction. He decided to collect the cash from the insurance policy and the sale of the house and leave the country. He would proclaim his need for a fresh start after the trauma of his wife's murder. His money would go a long way in Colombia or Ecuador, neither of which had extradition agreements with the United States, which left the issue of what to do with Pam.

He liked her and had planned to settle down with her, but now she was a liability as the only one who could tie him to the murders. Her participation in the theft of the medicines was minor enough that she could easily cut a deal with the authorities. He knew that Pam liked him, but doubted she loved him enough to sacrifice herself.

Unaware of himself as an organized psychopath, he simply solved problems, and sometimes other people's deaths effected the best solutions. He worked the problem, as he finished washing the deep punctures and tears with flaps of skin left to cover some of the wounds. He patted his arm dry and applied small dollops of superglue to the flaps to hold them in place, leaving openings to allow drainage. Sealing the wounds would significantly increase risk of infection. He wrapped his arm in gauze and searched his medicine cabinet for antibiotics. He took his first dose and decided his next move.

CHAPTER FORTY-FIVE

Wednesday, 11:14 p.m.

I arrived home to find that someone had bolted a piece of plywood over the broken glass door in back. I appreciated the neighborly favor and hoped they would watch my house. With Banshee on guard, I imagined that even a Navy Seal would find an undetected approach challenging.

Banshee alertly sniffed each room, wildly alarmed at the new diverse scents of everyone who had been in his domain. I let him outside, and he thoroughly investigated the backyard as well.

The large pieces of glass had been swept into the trash, but I noted that I needed to finish cleaning it in the morning. I reset my favorite chair on the porch at an angle to see anyone who might approach from either corner of the house. Banshee finished his securing of the perimeter, and we walked back inside together. I double checked that I had locked all the doors and windows and leaned my loaded shotgun against the night stand within easy reach. I could rack a shell, point, and shoot in a second, and the sound of a shell racking in a shotgun could inspire any intruder to reconsider his life choices.

I climbed into bed, and Banshee positioned himself next to me on the floor facing the door, as if daring the man to return. I cleared my mind and replayed the altercation for the thousandth time, reliving the helplessness of Banshee's unconsciousness and of his being trapped inside, followed by my elation at his awakening. I reheard the man's calm, measured words muffled by his mask. Finally, exhaustion drowned him out, and I surrendered to sleep.

CHAPTER FORTY-SIX

Thursday, 7:31 a.m.

David awoke invigorated by his dreamless slumber and new plans. With his wife's death certificate in hand, he called the life insurance company to cash out the policy as quickly as possible. The representative explained that they could expedite the process at a cost of one half percent of the policy amount, twenty thousand dollars. Though outraged, David was in no position to argue. He could stop by the office that morning, sign the paperwork, and deposit the cashier's check by noon the next day. The fee was worth it.

Next, he called one of a growing number of real estate investment groups that were quickly buying houses across the country. They paid cash for houses in any condition, but they offered about twenty percent less than what he could get on the open market. David didn't have months or even weeks to show the house. He agreed to meet their agent at noon to see the house and negotiate an offer. He figured the house was worth one point six million, and he would be lucky to get one point two, but combined with the proceeds from the life insurance, it wouldn't matter. If all went smoothly, he could disappear by Saturday, which meant he had one day to take care of Pam.

. . .

The monthly staff meeting with an administrator in the emergency department challenged us to find a reason to keep pumping blood to our brains during the mind-numbing hour and a half. Declared mandatory, or the administration would just as effectively speak to a vacant room, the meeting conveyed the same information every month, updated with new slides read aloud to us, followed by a summary of a new initiative designed to solve a nonexistent problem.

"Our new initiative is something we are really excited about. Anyone who picks up an extra shift in the emergency room will be entered into a raffle at the end of the month with a chance to win prizes, including a free lunch from the cafeteria, special parking up front for a day, or my favorite, having your picture hung on the wall as an 'Emergency Star Performer' for a whole week." Jan Ewing, a genuinely kind woman, was tasked with delivering inane messages to each department, not the worst job in the hospital, but only because someone had to clean the drains in the autopsy rooms. Fifty-five minutes into the meeting, she paused for questions. Dirk raised his hand.

"Great presentation and I love the new initiative that will no doubt inspire people to come in on their days off. Changing subjects, any thoughts on the recent murder epidemic in the hospital?"

"What do you mean?" Jan asked.

"Quality control reports are interesting, and who doesn't want to hear the latest stats on charting accuracy, but I thought maybe we could get an update on the murders of our colleagues. We've all been edgy under the additional grief and stress."

"I'm sorry. I don't have any more information than what has been in the news."

"Okay, maybe we could add it to next month's agenda, and admin can update whoever is still alive."

I kicked Dirk under the table, as poor Jan awkwardly concluded the meeting. Dirk wasn't wrong, but hospital administration would never work that way.

"You looking to stir up trouble, Dirk?"

"Just looking for some transparency. We've got five dead folks lying in the morgue, and a killer skipping through the hallways of our hospital. It seems like it should be addressed."

"How do you know he's skipping?"

"I assume so, because he has to be elated that he hasn't been arrested. I mean, how many people could be on the list of those who might seek revenge against five unrelated coworkers?"

I stopped in the hallway, as Dirk's words unlocked an elusive memory of the killer's words spoken while I coped with his gun pointed at my face. "Who says this is about vengeance?" He had said, when he had no reason to lie to me, which meant that the murders were not about revenge, which meant that everyone was looking at the wrong suspect pool. If not revenge, the next two most likely motives left sex and money.

"Dirk, you're a genius."

"Surprised it took you so long to figure that out."

"We've been misled the whole time. The killer made it seem like vengeance and framed Chuck beautifully, but he made a few small mistakes and one big one. He admitted to me that his murder spree was not about revenge."

"Then who should be on the list of possible suspects?"

"Whoever benefits from these murders."

"Who could possibly benefit from all this death? The mortician?"

"Yeah, but people always die. The funeral business always has new customers. No, we're looking for someone who benefitted directly. Think money and sex."

"I don't know about the sex part, but the three doctors and the CEO probably left behind some serious cash, maybe even enough to kill for."

I turned it over in my head. I had visited all three of the doctors' beautiful houses, and all three of their surviving spouses would have inherited them, plus any retirement accounts and insurance money.

"You know, Doc, only one of the victims was a woman."

"Yeah, Dr. Waverly, the anesthesiologist, but the killer could be a boyfriend of one of the other spouses."

"Yeah, after he attacked you, we know our killer is a dude, and we know he did it to benefit himself. Any boy toy wouldn't necessarily benefit directly, not like Waverly's husband, the other Dr. Waverly."

"Waverly does meet our criteria. He's male, average size, has access to all parts of the hospital, and potentially could access the medications. Plus, he would probably benefit financially from the death of his wife."

"Also, her murder was different, face to face and personal."

"In what way? Chuck and Guidry were, too."

"The other two doctors were killed remotely, though, and he had to set up the scene with the other two."

My whole body chilled. Waverly did check all the boxes, but a well respected physician turned serial killer strained credulity.

"You gonna tell the police?" Dirk asked.

"Not yet. I don't want to falsely accuse a grieving man of horrific crimes. If we're right, of course we tell the cops, but if I'm wrong, I don't want to ruin the guy's life even more than his wife's killer already has."

"Do you need my help?"

"I may, but for now, just keep this quiet while I do some research."

CHAPTER FORTY-SEVEN

Thursday, 10:53 a.m.

Waverly scowled, as he sacrificed another one and a half percent off the price of his house to have the funds expedited to his account within twenty-four hours. He consoled himself with the total amount that would leave him with the financial freedom to leave on Saturday, never to return to his country.

He shifted thoughts to his last issue. He could leave more quickly if he disappeared without dealing with Pam, but she could conclusively place him at every scene. On the other hand, with a new identity and residence in a non-extradition country, Pam's potential revelations may not matter.

His paranoia won. He would do it Friday night, because he had a last overnight shift beginning in a few hours and didn't want to draw attention to himself by not showing up. He could handle one last shift.

Waverly marveled at how easy killing had become. The first murder had taken months for him to commit to mentally, but efficient decisiveness preceded the subsequent killings. Perhaps pragmatism that five death sentences were equivalent to one as well as his lack of remorse had eased the process. Killing was simply a means to an end, like brushing his teeth.

Pam would need to be taken quietly and disposed of where she wouldn't be found for at least another day. His mind worked on a solution, the same way he diagnosed a complex patient, unaware of his untraceable transition into the realm of psychopathy.

.   .   .

Spike came through for me again. I asked her to dig up everything she could find on Waverly, particularly any links to any of the victims other than his wife. Waverly had gone to Notre Dame at the same time as Chuck Damon and had resided in the same dorm. It stood to reason that they had known each other, which gave a plausible explanation of how the list travelled from Chuck to Waverly.

Spike also discovered a life insurance policy on Waverly's wife worth four million dollars. People had killed their wives for a lot less.

The question of what to do with the information remained. Many couples maintained life insurance on each other, and the fact that he had gone to college with Chuck didn't mean that he had shot him, or even that he had gotten the list from him. My free pass with the detectives would expire at some point, and the way I got the information was shady at best. I was still determined not to ruin a guy whose wife had been murdered, if he had no part in it. I needed more before I went to the police with my suspicions, which begged the question of how to get such information. I could confront Waverly directly, disastrous if he were innocent and potentially dangerous if he were guilty. I considered sneaking into his house for a look around, but I doubted that someone smart enough to plan five murders that well would leave evidence lying around for me to find.

One more option occurred to me. The guy who attempted to kill me and murdered all five victims suffered from a fresh wound. If I could see the condition of his forearm, I could eliminate him as a suspect or confirm his identity as the killer. DNA would prove guilt or innocence, but at least I could give the police probable cause to obtain a sample. I finally fell asleep with no idea how to get a look at his forearm.

CHAPTER FORTY-EIGHT

Friday, 8:41 a.m.

No clever ideas came to me in my sleep, so I decided to go with the boring approach, surveillance. I didn't have the resources to follow him all day, but Spike had provided me with the license number, and I already had an extra tracker I had bought from Amazon months ago. I drove through the parking lot at the hospital and tucked the tracker under his bumper. The app would alert me when he moved. While I waited, I planned to satisfy my craving for Belgian waffles.

.   .   .

After his uneventful shift, Waverly drove home. The night shift had been so quiet that he had been able to sleep for a few hours. After a nap at home, he would feel well rested and ready to execute his plans.

The thought that this was his last day in the United States felt surreal. He had vacationed overseas, but had never spent much time out of the country. He had read about Ecuador, but the reality of living there would certainly be different. One thing for sure was that his money would go a long way down there.

He hoped both checks were ready on time. He would transfer all his money to his Bitcoin account and sell it as needed after his arrival in Ecuador. He already had a new identity prepared, and with no money trail, he would leave no way for anyone to track him down. Ecuador wouldn't extradite him, anyway.

He planned to cross the border to Mexico by car. From there, he would hire a small plane to fly to Ecuador to avoid customs. The authorities would focus on northbound traffic, not on people heading south, but he would pay cash and stay as unnoticeable as possible. After he established himself with his new identity, he could buy a house on the beach.

As he took care of his sleeping patients the night before, he had decided that Pam deserved a peaceful death. He really was fond of her and would like to travel with her, but he couldn't trust her to sever connections with her family. Eventually, she would call her mom or sister and shatter his carefully constructed anonymity. He would use the stun gun and fentanyl that had worked so well on his wife. The symmetry of their deaths pleased him.

For now, he had to get some sleep.

· · ·

After Waverly's drive home from the hospital, the next alert on the app came shortly after noon. It appeared that he went only to a bank for about twenty minutes before returning home.

The beautiful afternoon was unusually cool, so I took Banshee to the park with enough open space for him to run off leash. After heading back home, I fell asleep while reading on the couch and jolted awake from Banshee's snoring. Nothing happened on the app until after seven when Waverly got back into his car.

"Banshee, ready for another adventure?"

Banshee barked and swept his fluffy tail, dislodging another glass fragment. I carefully threw it in the trash and dressed him in his full tactical gear, including his vest with the ceramic plates that covered his staples.

•   •   •

Waverly whistled a meaningless tune, as he drove to Pam's house. He hadn't called first to avoid a digital trail that could lead back to him, not that it really mattered, as his own disappearance would be suspicious enough, but he saw no justification for imperfection.

He parked a couple doors down and walked nonchalantly to her front door. Excited to see him, she let him in after peeking out her window and enveloped him in a full body hug.

"How did everything go? Did you get the money?" she asked, as she held him tight.

"It went fine. The real estate and life insurance companies paid, and I transferred the funds to the crypto accounts. Are you still set on going to Brazil next week?" He hadn't ever mentioned Ecuador to her, in case she slipped and mentioned it to her family. He gave her a false timeline for the same reason.

"Of course. Are we still leaving on Thursday?"

"That's the plan. Why don't you get dressed? I have a surprise for you," David said.

"Are you in a rush, or do we have time for some fun?" Pam loosened her robe ties, revealing her nakedness underneath. David pushed the robe off her shoulders and followed her to the bedroom.

CHAPTER FORTY-NINE

Friday, 9:17 p.m.

Banshee and I arrived at the address indicated on the app a few minutes after Waverly's car had stopped in front of a small house beneath a shady ash tree. I drove further down the street with no way to know which house he was actually visiting and parked to leave myself a clear view of most of the area. I didn't want to get out and walk with Banshee looking especially distinctive in his tactical gear. Banshee irritably thumped his tail, but he eventually settled down across the backseat and rested his head.

"Relax, boy. You'll get your chance."

We waited about a half an hour before I watched him exit the house directly in front of where I had parked. I motioned to Banshee to remain still and silent and sank down in my seat.

I hadn't needed to worry. David focused only on the woman hanging on his arm, as they walked to his car. I immediately recognized Pam, the night nurse from the ICU. Another piece clicked into place, as I imagined David's seducing her to obtain the medications.

I considered calling the cops, but I still didn't have anything definitive enough for them to use, so I decided to follow them with the tracker's app.

.   .   .

"Where are we going, honey?" Pam asked.

"I told you. It's a surprise."

"Give me a hint."

"Okay. It's a romantic, once-in-a-lifetime experience."

Pam clasped her hands and grinned, as she anticipated David's proposal of marriage. Their relationship had started six months before, but they had worked together for years, as David routinely rounded on patients in the ICU. Charming and friendly, David had garnered many women's admiration, but David had always maintained only professional relationships with the staff.

One night, she needed a signature to release a patient's medicines from the pharmacy. She paged David, who said he needed a minute, as he had just settled into his call room. In a hurry, Pam offered to run to his room to get his signature. She had expected nothing more, but when he opened the door, he seemed to acknowledge the hungry expression in her eyes with his own desirous gaze. He signed the form, and Pam made the first move with a tentative kiss that had intensified into an affair.

Pam had dressed quickly to rush back to work that night and had avoided any potential awkwardness at the end of their initial sexual encounter. Obsessed with him through the rest of her shift, she had found him waiting for her outside the ICU. They had talked easily for over an hour over breakfast. David had explained his growing distance from his wife and his plan to leave her.

Pam had listened without recognizing her position as the mistress who would doom the marriage. She had figured that David deserved happiness, and if his wife couldn't meet his needs, then she would. They had agreed to keep their relationship secret and had stolen time together when they could. David had visited her house before and after his shifts.

She had never tried to recall when he had first advanced the idea of stealing narcotics nor did she define it that way to herself. He had originally broached the topic that he could frame his wife for skimming patients' prescriptions for pain control in order to give himself a socially acceptable reason to divorce her. At some point, the plan had evolved to include murder. By then, Pam had already stolen the drugs and thought only about spending the rest of her life in utter happiness with David. He bolstered his reasoning for the additional murders by sharing the terrible things that those doctors, including his wife, had done. He had explained that they needed the money from her life insurance to build their own life together. Pam justified his actions with a healthy dose of denial combined with her obsessive infatuation with him. She distanced herself from responsibility for the killings by assuring herself that she wasn't hurting anyone through her own actions and that the victims were bad people anyway.

Pam closed her eyes and imagined her idealized new life married to David. Brazil was exotic, and he had promised her a house on the beach where they could raise a family.

.   .   .

"Where the hell are they going?" I asked Banshee.

He tilted his head, trying to understand.

They headed northwest from Phoenix, and there isn't much out there, other than Las Vegas, a five-hour drive away. I was considering abandoning the trip, when they exited Route 93 and turned onto a road that didn't appear to have a name. They headed west toward Alamo Lake State Park, driving through largely empty areas.

My reception was already spotty and would worsen, as we entered the mountainous region further from civilization. Soon, I would lose the ability to track them. I sped up to close the distance and spotted their brake lights, the only lights visible, a few miles ahead of me. The dusty tail from their passing marked their path. I turned off my lights to avoid being seen. We were the only cars around, and it wouldn't take much thought for them to figure out that they were being followed.

A full moon and a clear sky of stars illuminated the road fairly well after my eyes adjusted. I cut my following distance in half and focused on the road.

Banshee still gazed at me in wonder. I love that dog and thought again about how lucky I was to have him.

CHAPTER FIFTY

Friday, 11:43 p.m.

David didn't have a specific destination in mind, as long as the area was remote enough that her body wouldn't be found for at least a day. Convinced of their isolation in the middle of nowhere, he took a right and drove up a narrow dirt track to the summit of a small, flat hill with a commanding view of the surrounding terrain and the constellations above. He turned off the car and mentally prepared to kill her, but she had other plans.

"Oh, baby, this is beautiful. We've never fucked under the stars before."

"I have an old blanket in the trunk. You choose some music from my playlist."

David smoothed the blanket across the ground, while Pam restarted the car and chose jazz to play through the speakers. She approached David, dropping her clothes, as she walked to sit on the blanket next to him.

The exotic surroundings fueled passionate sex. At the moment of climax, David injected her with a full syringe of fentanyl. Surprised, Pam's eyes pooled with fearful tears, as she felt the first sensations of the fentanyl and comprehension panicked her. The drugs coursed through her rapidly, turning her despair to euphoria and then nothingness.

David watched the light in her eyes dim and felt nothing other than satisfaction of completion of another step. Pam could no longer cause a problem. He kissed her forehead and left her partially covered with the blanket. With Pam already forgotten, he considered the next step of his travel plans, as he dressed and drove away from the desolate hill.

.   .   .

I watched the car climb a small hill and stop at the top, parked my car behind some brush around the far side of the hill, and turned my engine off. We stepped out of the car and gently closed the door. I couldn't see them, but heard music playing. I motioned for Banshee to stay quiet, as we began the easy climb up the backside of the hill. We had to move slowly to avoid noise from the crackling of the dry underbrush. I marveled at Banshee's ability to stalk in silence.

Staying low to the ground, we reached the rim of the plateau and peeked over the edge. Pam and David were wrapped together in a blanket, as music played from the car. Never a voyeur, I lowered my head to back away, when David stood up from the blanket and reached for his clothes. Thick white gauze covered his right forearm, confirming that he had attacked Banshee and me. He dressed, while Pam continued to rest.

David casually walked to the driver's side, and to my surprise, he climbed in and drove away. Pam didn't move. My heart sank, and I moved to check on her, calling her name. I rushed to her side and felt for a pulse, only to find none. I performed CPR for two minutes, but I knew my efforts were hopeless. I had no medicine, no defibrillator, and no help. Pam was gone, and there was nothing I could do to save her.

I had to decide whether to take her with me or leave her in place. Taking her seemed more humane, but I knew I would destroy more evidence than I already had. Leaving her alone up there pained me, but I rationalized that she could feel no discomfort now, and I would call for help as soon as I could connect to a cell tower. I wrapped her tightly in the blanket in a meek effort to honor her dignity, although I knew the detectives probably wouldn't appreciate it, then ran back to my car. Banshee jumped in first, and I drove as fast as I safely could, anxious to get the authorities on sight before any wild animals disturbed her.

.   .   .

David, who had pulled over to relieve himself, startled at the roar of a car racing through the desert night from the emptiness behind him. As he tried to make sense of this apparition about to appear from nowhere, he hurriedly pulled his car off the road to park within a copse of scraggly mesquite that hopefully rendered his car invisible from the road. He crept back toward the roar of the engine to glimpse the other car as it passed. The speeding dark sedan, probably a Mercedes, did not reveal the driver, but a German Shepherd's head hung out the window, his snout sniffing in the wind.

Stunned, David analyzed how the hell that doctor had followed him all the way out here. He hadn't seen anyone in his mirrors, and he hadn't even known exactly where he was going when he had left Phoenix. That doctor from emergency room must have tracked him somehow.

He frantically searched his vehicle to find the tracker. He pulled it off and prepared to throw it into the wasteland behind him, when a better idea occurred to him. He took his car back onto the road and turned north with the tracker on the seat beside him.

Twenty minutes later, he reached a gas station, where a red Mustang pulled up to the pump next to him, and a couple raced inside, as another man started to pump the gas, and yelled at the couple to hurry up so they could start winning in Vegas. David attached the tracker to their wheel well and took off toward Phoenix.

The driver of the Mustang finished pumping the gas, as the couple raced back out to the vehicle. Soon, they headed north toward Las Vegas, unaware of how exciting their trip was about to become.

CHAPTER FIFTY-ONE

Saturday, 12:29 a.m.

I finally reached the main road and received a solid signal on my phone. I pulled over to call Detective Frist, who answered in a voice that made it clear she had been asleep.

"This is Frist. Who's this?"

"Doc from the emergency room. David Waverly is the killer, and he just murdered another woman."

"Slow down, Doc, and start making sense." Frist sat up in bed, fully awake, and opened her journal to take notes.

I organized my thoughts better to explain my actions, beginning with my following Waverly to Pam's house and ending with Pam's death on top of the hill. Frist listened without interruption.

"Do you still have a signal on Waverly's location?" she asked.

I opened my app to see him moving northwest. "Yes, he's headed toward Las Vegas about twenty miles north of me."

"Stay right there. I'm gonna figure out who the local authorities are and meet you out there. We need you to take us to the murder scene. I'll get highway patrol to be on the lookout for his car and stop him. Let me know if he turns off the main road."

Relieved to have done what I could, I leaned my seat back and rested, while I awaited their arrival. Banshee whimpered, and I got out of the car to let him out. I knew he could take care of himself, and he could stretch his legs while I rested. Every few minutes, I checked the app and watched the blue dot progress steadily northwest.

I wondered what inspired a man, especially an otherwise respected physician, to become a killer. He had taken an oath to do no harm and to help people, and by all accounts, he had been an excellent doctor for many years. Maybe he had succumbed to mental illness that he had suppressed for years. Maybe he had succumbed merely to greed. Whatever the case, he had ruined the lives of the victims as well as those of their loved ones. Six families and groups of friends would have to learn to live without them and cope with grief, a demon I had not shaken off myself, that soft voice in the back of my mind pointed out.

The local Sheriff arrived first. In his forties, he had clearly spent more time sitting in his car and eating fast food than exercising and eating healthfully. He carried about fifty extra pounds that challenged the strength of the buttons on his shirt. His belt worked overtime to keep his gear in place, as he lumbered toward my car.

"You Docker?" he asked.

"Yes, sir. I assume you're the local Sheriff."

"I'm in charge out here, but as you can see, there ain't much to be in charge of. I was told we have a dead body in the hills."

"Yes, sir. Do you want me to take you there?"

"Let's sit tight until the detectives get here. It sounds like it's gonna be their case, and I don't have the resources for a murder investigation, anyway. Holy shit!" He started reaching for his gun, but I held out my hand to stop him.

"Relax, Sheriff, that's my dog." Banshee materialized silently from the shadows, sat at my side, and peered at the Sheriff with innocent eyes.

"Damn thing about gave me a heart attack."

I didn't point out that he was about one sneeze away from a heart attack already and scratched Banshee behind the ears.

"Sorry about that, Sheriff. He tends to move stealthily."

A siren broke into our small talk, followed by red and blue flashing lights, as Frist and Teamont pulled up on the other side of my car. Introductions were made, and Frist took charge.

"Let me see Waverly's current location."

I handed her my phone, and she communicated the location to law enforcement up the road.

"We need to keep them updated on the location," she said.

"We can do better. Have them download the app, and I'll give them my password, so that they can login and watch it in real time."

Frist passed on the information, and after the police had the app live, she asked me to lead them to Pam's body. Frist rode with me, while Teamont and the Sheriff followed in their own cars.

"I thought I told you to leave the investigating to us," she reminded me, as we drove through the lonely landscape.

"I had planned to. I wanted to confirm my suspicions about Waverly before I set you guys loose on him. I would feel horrible if I falsely accused an innocent man. I didn't expect to follow him to a murder scene."

"Fair enough. At least the story makes sense now. He had an affair with Pam, who helped him get the meds. Unfortunately for her, Dr. Waverly has no issues with killing the women in his life."

"I also learned that Waverly went to college at Notre Dame at the same time as Chuck did, and they lived in the same dorm. There's your connection between Waverly and the list."

"Hell, Doc. I might have this whole thing wrapped up by the morning. The state police are closing in on his car; you can put him at the murder scene for Pam; and after we start digging into those leads, maybe we can tie him to the other murders, too. It'll be a long night, but I do appreciate your calling me, Doc."

The trip lasted only fifteen minutes, driving with my lights on this time. The tracks we had left earlier led a clear path back to Pam's body. Frist asked me to park at the bottom of the hill to avoid further contamination of the crime scene. We prepared to walk up to the body, and Sheriff Henderson volunteered to remain with the cars. Banshee scouted ahead and confirmed that no one else was around.

Pam's body remained wrapped in the blanket, as I had left her, with the infinite beauty of the starry skies and dark desert landscape contrasting starkly with the ugliness of the crime. I pointed to the tracks where Waverly had parked his car and to my prior vantage point at the edge of the plateau. They took it all in and Frist led us back to the bottom of the hill, where our cars remained safe, thanks to Sheriff Henderson.

Frist used her radio to learn the location of her evidence team, bumping along on the dirt road, about ten minutes away. Turning her attention to the hunt for Waverly, she called the state police. Scowling, she stepped back out of her vehicle.

"The good news is that the state police located the tracker and pulled the car over. The bad news is that Waverly wasn't in it. Sounds like they stopped for gas, where Waverly must have moved the tracker to their Mustang headed to Vegas."

"If he pointed us north, then he's probably headed south," I said.

"Dammit! We don't know that. He probably just stuck it on the most convenient car," Frist said, as she grabbed her radio to alert Phoenix units to be on the lookout for Waverly, possibly armed and dangerous, with a description of his car. Next, she called Border Patrol to ask them to watch for him at the crossings. Chasing fugitives south of the border was costly, dangerous, and often futile.

I watched the evidence team arrive for the grisly job of documenting the murder and collecting evidence. Sheriff Henderson, asleep in his car, left Banshee and me to ourselves until Frist returned. She shook her head at the sleeping Sheriff.

"I'm concerned about his health," I said.

"Hopefully, he isn't destined for a visit to the emergency room any time soon. Can you give me a ride back to town, please? Teamont will stay with the body, while I coordinate the search for Waverly."

I held open the passenger door, and Banshee jumped in first. He hopped into the back, when he realized that Frist needed the passenger seat. Banshee stretched across the back seat, and inspired by Sheriff Henderson, quickly fell asleep.

"What do you think Waverly is gonna do?" I asked.

"If he found the tracker, then he knows he was followed, which means he knows he has a target on his back, which means it's time to run. If he's smart, which he has been so far, he'll head for the border. If he crosses, he can disappear with his money."

"Think they'll get him at the border?"

"Better than even odds, I think. Border Patrol is really good when they have a specific target."

"Let's hope so. I don't think we can be sure that he won't kill again."

With that thought, we drove in heavy silence toward the lights of Phoenix.

CHAPTER FIFTY-TWO

Saturday, 1:36 a.m.

Fifteen miles ahead, Waverly crossed into city limits. His blinding fury had settled to smoldering rage in which he could think more clearly. Now that he was on the run, the police would be on the lookout for him and his car. He parked it at a strip mall that featured a men's club, a twenty-four-hour liquor store, a tattoo parlor, and a check-cashing business with metal bars behind grimy windows and left the keys on the dash. He used his key card from the hospital to unscrew his license plate and pitched it into a dumpster a block away.

He jogged twenty minutes to the storage unit he had leased under a fake name, where he had stowed what he needed to disappear. He opened the lock, turned on the light, and closed the rolling door behind him.

The first order of business was to change his appearance. He shaved his thin beard and mowed his hair down to a crew cut with a cordless hair clipper. He added a magnetic gold stud to one ear and gold wire framed glasses. He added a worn black baseball cap, trendy faded jeans, black cowboy boots, and a black t-shirt.

He had already backed in a ten-year-old white pickup truck he had bought with cash from an online ad months ago. Inside, his suitcase contained four sets of clothes and his new identity as well as another taser and a pistol. Now named Jim Mullen with a driver's license, credit card, and passport, he felt confident that the exorbitantly expensive documents would stand up to scrutiny.

He had to cross the border, which he knew would be on heightened alert for at least the next few days, as the cops almost certainly anticipated that he might flee the country. Phoenix offered relatively few roads out of town, which simplified the police's task to watch all of them. The smart play would be to hole up in town until the search for him cooled off.

He drove away from the storage unit after pulling down its door for the last time. His destination was a hotel that catered to temporary workers by offering weekly rates and a discount for cash. Not the type to verify identities, the clerk slid a key across the counter without bothering to look at him.

The depressingly dank and dimly lit room featured only a lumpy bed, an ancient boxy television, and a minimal bathroom of questionable cleanliness. A sickening scent of cigarette smoke permeated the room. A dingy diner next door promised greasy fare, and he had noted a vending machine with drinks, chips, and candy on the way to his room. He could survive a few days before beginning his journey south.

With clarity to think now that his anger had boiled down to a simmer, he considered going after Doc, who he blamed for his current predicament and who had the nerve to follow him like that. The idea of vengeance restored his sense of control but introduced additional risky complications. Without Doc's interference, he would have been on a plane to South America much sooner. Instead, he had to endure this shit hole, and his delayed trip would pose more challenges. He ruminated his options until exhaustion overtook him.

. . .

Border crossings from California to Texas had reported no sign of Waverly and neither had local police. News sites circulated his picture throughout their morning news cycles, but no credible leads had materialized. Waverly had disappeared.

His home and office, searched extensively, disgorged nothing relevant. DNA samples had been collected and submitted for comparison to the blood collected at Doc's house, but those results would take another day.

Armed with search warrants, Frist and Teamont had accessed his accounts to learn of the significant fees he had paid to expedite the payments for the sale of his house and for the proceeds from the life insurance as well as his quick transfer of the total to cryptocurrency. The crypto account defied their attempts to trace the money.

Interviews with neighbors and coworkers expressed disbelief that Waverly could be a serial killer, although some of his coworkers acknowledged that they could see it in hindsight.

"Do you think we missed him at the border, or do you think he's hiding locally?" Teamont asked.

"I don't think we missed him. We had the word out before he could possibly get close to the border, and their technology makes it difficult to pass when a specific target is identified. I don't think he moved north given the few roads with officers on all of them. I think he's still here somewhere, waiting for the heat to die down," Frist said.

"The reward money is up to $100,000, and the amateur sleuths are surely headed this way for a shot at the jackpot."

"He's smart. He's bold. He's a planner. Our identifying him before he left the country has got to be frustrating for him. Assuming he is frustrated, do you think he'll make a mistake?"

"Maybe. Guys like that think they're invincible, so any failure could send him over the edge."

"Do you think he'll have another go at Doc?"

"Possibly. It would be stupid, but the risk might be worth it to him."

"I agree. Let's give Doc a heads up, and we can park a car on his street. I wish he would just let us put him in a hotel under a pseudonym."

.   .   .

Antsy in his hotel room, Waverly was a man of action, and sitting around to wait for everyone to calm down was not in his nature. He needed to do something, and his first preference was to obtain the catharsis of ridding his world of Doc.

With the dusky light fading to darkness, he decided to do a little reconnaissance. Unconcerned about being identified with his disguise and his old truck, he still made sure to drive perfectly to avoid an accident or a traffic stop. He tuned out the country music station playing softly in the background and imagined that every set of eyes scrutinized and accused him. In actuality, no one paid him even a cursory glance.

The neat sidewalks of the quiet neighborhood hosted only a few late evening residents out for a stroll. Waverly turned onto Doc's street and tensed at the sight of a police car parked in front of the house. He continued down the street to pull up next to the car and saw the officer inside busy on his phone. He briefly raised his head to nod at the passing truck and returned to his screen. Waverly drove past and inhaled deeply to slow his quickened heart rate.

Even though the guard failed to intimidate, his presence effectively conveyed that the house was not a viable target. He didn't fear the cop, but he did fear the radio that could summon immediate help. Waverly drove out of the neighborhood from its opposite side feeling even more frustrated. By the time he was back at the irritating hotel, he had formulated a better plan.

CHAPTER FIFTY-THREE

Saturday, 7:53 p.m.

The overnight shift sucks. Some distant descendants of vampires might disagree, but for the majority of people, night shifts suck. The pay is a little better, and the patient volumes are usually lower, but I would be on my own, and if things went bad, no one would come to my aid.

There is also the issue of circadian rhythms. People are wired to wake up in the morning and to sleep at night. When we try to reverse that, it screws up our natural cycles of mental alertness. Most hospitals schedule three or four night shifts in a row to offer the chance to adjust. That's thoughtful, except that in three or four days, you have to adjust back to a traditional schedule.

After I signed into my first night shift of the month, the doctor ending his shift left me five patients in various stages of work up. Transfers of patients from one doctor to the next are not ideal care, but they're necessary. Some of these patients may not have a disposition for another eight hours, and the original doctor can't stay all night waiting for results.

Added to the group of patients who had already been seen was a substantial list of people waiting to see a doctor. Evening is one of the busiest times in the emergency room. Everyone wanted to be seen before they planned to go to bed, and all of the drinkers and drug users would be out making bad choices. The chaos would continue until past midnight, when the last remaining doctor besides myself would leave, and hopefully, the emergency room would be cleared out by four. At six, the process would start over again with the early birds checking into the emergency room for evaluation. This never-ending cycle of people visiting the emergency room is as predictable and as unpredictable as the tides.

I introduced myself to the patients who had been checked out to me, then picked up my first chart on a twenty-five-year-old drunk who came in for evaluation after a fight outside a bar. Unsurprisingly, he had a swollen hand with significant pain around his pinky finger. Delicate hand bones don't react well to smashing into solid objects like skulls. I put on my game face and entered the room.

.   .   .

Waverly's heart rate escalated with the thrill of anticipation. His determination to target Doc had implanted so deeply into his crazed mind that he couldn't eliminate the idea, even if he had wanted to, and he didn't want to. He wanted Doc dead, and if he had the chance, he would kill that vicious dog, too, but as long as he achieved Doc's death, he would satisfy the insistent voices in his head.

Going after Doc at the hospital was either brilliant or idiotic, or maybe a combination of both. Waverly, well aware of his current infamy and the fact that many people at the hospital would recognize him, correctly surmised that even so, no one would be looking for him there. None would expect that of all places he could be implementing his next move, the hospital would be a potential choice, but it made perfect sense to him. His killing spree started with a doctor's dramatic death in the hospital and would end with another.

Access to the hospital was too easy. He had scanned his old badge into a computer, updated the name and photo, and printed and laminated a new one. It would not work to open protected doors, but when hung from a lanyard around his neck, it would fool anyone who bothered to look. Betting that the hospital had not disabled his original badge yet and wouldn't be monitoring it either, he carried it in his pocket in case he needed it to open a secured door.

He parked in the garage, hung his badge around his neck, and walked in the front door with confidence in his adequate disguise. His backpack hung from his shoulder. The security guard in the lobby didn't give him a second glance. He took the stairs to the basement, quiet at this hour, and found a cleaning cart stored in the hallway, waiting for the next day's employee. He pushed it ahead of him, knowing that the cleaning crew accessed all parts of the hospital at all hours, usually with no set schedule, and no one thought twice about their presence.

The cleaning cart had the added advantage of holding his backpack out of sight. He settled it under some trash bags with the zipper open for easy access and began his unofficial rounds of the hospital.

Pretending to be a cardiologist who wanted to discuss a patient, he had called the emergency room earlier to ascertain that Doc was working. The receptionist had kindly informed him that Doc had the overnight shift, which was perfect for his plans.

Unnoticed in the crowded department, he made only one pass through the emergency room and saw Doc and his dog walking in the hall between patients. With confirmation of his presence, Waverly headed back to the lower level of the hospital to prepare. He would come for Doc later, when he would least expect it.

CHAPTER FIFTY-FOUR

Sunday, 3:47 a.m.

Typically, people hit a wall of fatigue between three and four in the morning, and I slammed into it at about 3:30, after I discharged my last active patient from the emergency room. Five patients remained to wait on lab results or for a consult to see them in a few hours, but no new patients waited to be seen. Adrenaline levels that had fueled the first two thirds of my shift abruptly fell, and the familiar, unpleasant exhaustion of sleep deprivation caught up to me.

"Strong work, Doc, the board is clear," Dirk said. He seemed bestowed with unlimited energy, even on night shifts.

"Thanks for your help. I need to take Banshee outside and then hopefully, close my eyes for a few minutes."

"Go ahead and grab a call room, and I'll take care of Banshee. I would love to step outside for a bit."

I shook my head in amazement, as I watched Banshee and Dirk walk out the back door. They had to be the only two left in the hospital with any energy at this hour. My stomach rumbled, and I leveraged myself out of my chair and told the nurses I was headed out to grab something to eat and to text me if they needed me. Murphy's Law dictated that the sickest person would arrive during the three minutes I stepped out of the emergency room.

I stretched my back, then headed to the cafeteria through a long hallway, empty except for a lone janitor, busy with mopping an already shiny floor. Closed at that hour, the cafeteria offered only a row of vending machines. I passed the ones filled with healthier options and stopped in front of the machine featuring pop-tarts and chips. The sugar and the salt sounded good, so I bought one of each, swiped them from the low tray, and turned to bump into the janitor. I hadn't heard his approach.

"Excuse me," I said.

He pulled a gun from his cart. "I don't think so, Doc. You're coming with me."

I blinked, as my sleep deprived brain took an extra moment to process the nonsensical situation of a hospital janitor holding me at gun point by a vending machine in the middle of the night.

"You don't recognize me, do you? Funny, since you got half the state out looking for me," the man said.

Dread filled me, as I realized who he was. "Dr. Waverly, I see you are returning to the scene of your crimes. I assume you are not here to confess your sins and turn yourself in."

"Hardly. I want answers from you, but not here. Head to the stairs, and do what I say, or I'll shoot you and three more people in the emergency room. You don't want that on your conscience."

I certainly didn't, and I knew this madman was capable of carrying out the threat. I decided to cooperate. I gently placed my snacks in the side pockets of my white coat and wrapped my right hand around a needle I had dropped into the pocket from an earlier procedure. I uncapped it and poked my finger hard enough to draw blood and smeared my hand on a table next to me.

"Let's go, Doc. We're taking the stairs down. Don't try anything. I want answers, but I don't need them, so follow my directions."

I turned toward the stairway, opened the door, and left another smear of blood on the handle.

"The police figured you would run for the border."

"Of course they did. That's why I didn't do it."

"Why did you kill all those people? Was it really just about the money?"

"The money was a bonus. All of those people were scum who dishonored our profession."

"Your actions haven't exactly brought honor to the field of medicine."

That comment brought a tap from the gun on the top of my head. "Shut the fuck up. No more talking until I ask you a question."

We proceeded in silence. I held onto the railing on the way downstairs, leaving a bloody trail. In the basement, he had me turn right, and I moved to the side of the hall to reach some equipment stored there and brush my bleeding finger against everything I could. He pointed me toward the pathology area and forced me into the autopsy lab.

"Now you are about to be the star of my final act in this hospital." I turned to face him, and fifty thousand volts spread through my body, and I collapsed on the hard, frigid floor.

.   .   .

"Anybody seen Doc?" Dirk's deep voice rumbled through the quiet emergency room. A chorus of negative responses from the sleepy staff contrasted with a lone voice that informed him of Doc's quest for a snack.

"C'mon, Banshee. Let's get one, too."

Banshee pranced beside Dirk, as they walked through the vacant hallway and found the vending area equally deserted.

"Where the hell did you disappear to, Doc?" Dirk spun in place, trying to figure out which call room Doc may have found. Someone would have seen him duck into one in the emergency department, and he certainly would have told someone, in case they had to wake him up. Dirk checked a restroom nearby, also vacant.

Meanwhile, Banshee sniffed the perimeter and startled Dirk, when his bark at the door to the stairwell echoed through the empty hall.

"What's wrong, boy?"

Banshee whimpered and pawed at the door.

"You want to go in the staircase?"

Banshee stood on his back feet and pressed his paws on the door.

"Okay. We can take a look."

Dirk opened the door, and Banshee rushed inside, furiously sniffed the railing, and bounded down the stairs. Dirk chased the anxious dog and grew increasingly concerned, as he had never seen Banshee panic. At the bottom of the stairs, Banshee pressed his snout against a door handle where Dirk noticed fresh blood.

"Okay, Banshee, we'll find him, but we need to be QUIET." Dirk tried to say it like Doc did, and Banshee stilled, as Dirk opened the door to a long, dimly lit hallway, empty except for shadows cast by stored equipment.

"Nothing bad ever happens in creepy hospital basements, right Banshee?"

Banshee turned confidently to the right, as Dirk jogged to catch up.

"Banshee, SLOW, HUNT." He snuck like a feral apex predator, as he crept low and silently down the hall and blended into the shadows.

CHAPTER FIFTY-FIVE

Sunday, 4:11 a.m.

Waverly struggled to get my inert form off the floor and onto a pathology table. Moving 190 pounds of limp body weight is a physical feat, and bewilderment by his possible reasoning for this effort flitted across my exhausted mind. My muscles were still unresponsive, as he finally got my upper body on the table and swung my legs around to complete his unnecessary task. As I tried to move my arms, he hit me with another shock from the stun gun. He bound my arms and legs to the table with zip ties and pulled them tight enough that I had no chance of moving, even if I could. He stuck a piece of tape to my cheek but didn't pull it across my mouth. Apparently, he wanted to talk and waited patiently for normal function to return to my muscles.

"Sorry about that. I'm sure it's unpleasant."

"I'd be happy to demonstrate the stun gun on you and let you decide for yourself how unpleasant it is." My voice sounded weak, as I struggled to form words.

His cold, uncaring eyes calculated an apparent response. "Before I begin, I want to know why you wouldn't let this go. Why did you stay focused on me, even after everyone else was ready to accept that Damon was the killer?"

"I took it personally when three of my patients, three colleagues from this hospital, died in front of me. Three people, who had devoted their lives to helping others, were senselessly murdered in a place of healing."

"Their murders weren't senseless."

"Maybe not to you, but I spoke with the two widows and saw the pain those deaths caused. Those people didn't have to die and certainly not in such horrible ways. You're just a crazy murderer, no better than any other violent convict in prison, where you will soon reside, too."

"My version of this saga ends differently. I'll be on a beach surrounded by beautiful women and living a life of luxury. Let's focus on how your story ends. This all began with a spectacular death of a doctor in this hospital and will end with one, as well. I plan to do an autopsy on you, removing all of your organs and leaving them on the table beside you. I am curious how many organs I can remove before you bleed out."

"You're a sick fuck."

"That's not even the best part. When all of the organs are out, I am going to cut your head off, and place it on your chest facing the door. The first person in the door tomorrow will be in for the surprise of their life, truly a memory they won't forget."

I struggled at my bonds, as I saw complete derangement in his eyes, and fear overcame me. Waverly laughed softly, as he watched my futile efforts to free myself, and he scanned my body, as if he considered where to begin.

All I could think of was Banshee. "HELP!"

Waverly guffawed, as he pulled the tape across my mouth and turned to pick up a scalpel from the counter.

·　　·　　·

Banshee heard the cry for help and burst through the swinging doors with his teeth bared and instantly registered Doc's vulnerable position on the table, as well as the scent of the man who had hurt him and who now stood over Doc with something shiny and metal in his hand. Banshee launched.

.   .   .

I watched Waverly's confusion turn to horror, as my own avenging angel attacked suddenly and overwhelmingly. Banshee's jaws clamped down on the same forearm he had mangled days before. With unrelenting pressure on Waverly's arm, Banshee vigorously shook his head. Waverly's scream drowned out Banshee's growl, but amazingly, he remained on his feet.

A shadow fell across me, as Dirk rushed into the room. In two strides, he was at my side with his arm already moving forward, as he leaned over me. His oversized fist struck Waverly in his temple and twisted his head violently to the side. Waverly, knocked out cold by the blow, fell to the floor. I recognized a severe concussion, and I wouldn't have been surprised if he had a brain bleed.

Dirk ripped the tape off my mouth. "Who is that?!"

"That's Waverly, the killer. Banshee, STOP!" I could hear Banshee's wet gnawing and growling. I heard him shake his head again unknowing whether he had let go yet. He jumped up on the bed to give me kisses, and I tried my best to turn away from his bloody snout, while I told him to jump down and guard. Dirk grabbed another scalpel from the counter to free me.

I sat up and massaged my chafed wrists. "Did I ever mention how much I hate night shifts?"

"Did I ever mention how much I hate creepy hospital basements at night? What's the plan here?"

"Find some bandages and dress that arm wound, but leave him in place. I'm afraid you may have broken his neck with that punch."

"That was just a little love tap."

"Call it what you want, but that did some damage. Call the emergency room, and get them down here with a stretcher, backboard, and C-collar. I'll call the cops."

I decided to bypass 911 and called Frist directly. Her sleepy voice answered after four rings.

"This better be important."

"Sorry to wake you. It's Doc. Waverly just tried to kill me again, but Dirk knocked him out, and Banshee is guarding him."

A much more alert voice responded. "Where are you?"

"We're at the hospital in the pathology lab, but we're moving him to the emergency room for a CT scan and neck X-rays."

"Don't let him go anywhere. I'm on my way, and I'll be sending a bunch more people."

"I wouldn't worry about him escaping. He probably won't even be awake for a while. See you soon."

I disconnected and hugged Banshee. "You're such a good boy. You found the trail I left for you, didn't you?"

"He certainly did. He went crazy when he smelled the blood and led me here. So this is the little punk that killed all those people? I should have punched him a couple of weeks ago, and we could have prevented all that."

"Everything's clear in hindsight. Let's get him upstairs and get ready for the cops. They're gonna have a few questions."

Voices approached from down the hall. With nothing happening in the emergency room, nine people had journeyed downstairs, about six more than we needed. They got Waverly secured in a neck brace, placed on a backboard, and moved to the emergency room. A nurse handed me a warm, wet washcloth and suggested that I wipe the blood off my face. I thanked her and scrubbed my face and then Banshee's. Once we were both reasonably clean, I followed them back upstairs.

In the trauma room, I began my assessment like I would for any other patient, focusing on airway, breathing, and circulation.

"Kind of weird taking care of a guy who tried to kill you," Dirk said.

"He was a killer down there, but here, he's just a patient with a head injury. Let's get baseline labs, neck X-rays, and a CT scan of the head. Start some antibiotics for that arm wound, and let's get it flushed out. Surgery can deal with it once we know the extent of his head injury."

Results materialized quickly, as Waverly was our only active patient. Neck X-rays were normal, but he remained in a neck collar until he awakened and could follow commands. The CT scan of the head did not show evidence of a fracture or bleed, which surprised me and reminded me that a human body can miraculously tolerate a lot of trauma.

When the police arrived, Waverly was regaining consciousness, groggy but attempting to focus on his surroundings. He soon figured out that he had not been napping on a beach. The first officers to arrive had cuffed him to the bed, although he was probably physically incapable of fleeing.

Teamont beat Frist to the emergency room by a couple of minutes. They evaluated Waverly lying in bed with a large bruise and significant swelling developing on the side of his face.

"Is he gonna live?" Frist asked.

"He has no head bleed or neck injury, but probably a bad concussion. He'll need to be monitored for at least twenty-four hours until his neuro status improves, and he'll need surgery to repair his arm, but he'll make it."

"Okay. Tell me what happened, Doc."

I shared my story, and Dirk told a better, more animated and detailed one. We led them to the pathology lab, and I pointed out the areas where I had left a bloody trail and pledged to myself to clean it up after they finished their evidence collection. We ended up encircling the pathology table, where I had almost been eviscerated.

"Hell of a night, Doc," Frist said.

"Memorable for sure. I'll leave you guys to do your thing. I have some charting to complete and then I'm going home for a long shower and a nap."

"After the nap, we need you down at the station for a full interview."

"Deal."

"Hey, I'm not in trouble for hitting that guy, am I?" Dirk asked.

"I think we'll pass on filing assault charges at this time," Frist said.

"That's good. I don't think I would do well on a prison diet."

Frist looked him up and down. "I'm not sure how you can survive on any diet. Get out of here, and let us get to work, and thanks for knocking him out."

"Any time, Officer. Any time."

CHAPTER FIFTY-SIX

Sunday, 11:15 a.m.

After a three-hour nap and a quick sandwich, Banshee and I sat down with the detectives for a formal interview. It seemed like I had spent more time talking with the police than with coworkers lately. The discussion was relatively brief, as they already had most of the details. Finally, they finished and turned off the recorders.

"Has he said anything?" I asked.

"We haven't tried to speak with him yet. Between the anesthesia and the head injury, he's not fully aware and able to understand his rights. Anything he says at the moment may not be admissible. We'll read him his rights again after he wakes up completely and then begin the questioning," Frist said.

"Do you have enough to convict him?"

"A first year law student could convict him on the two attempted murder charges against you and the murder charge for Pam's homicide. The others are mostly circumstantial at the moment, but we can go back and review video and badge swipes to place him near the scene of all three crimes. Between that and what he said to you in the pathology lab, we can tie him to all of the murders."

"Good. I don't want him sneaking up on me again, and I damn sure don't want him tasing me again. Takes a week to fully recover from getting zapped by that thing."

"His days of tasing people are over. Thanks for your help, Doc. Looks like you'll have to go back to medicine and leave the investigating to us."

"I'm fine with that. Emergency medicine is a lot less dangerous than your job. Be careful out there."

Banshee and I left the police station, hopefully for the last time.

CHAPTER FIFTY-SEVEN

Three Weeks Later

"That was a quiet shift. No one punched, kicked, or spit on me today," Dirk said, as he sat down at the table with Sue and me. The mostly empty diner had already cleared the dinner crowd.

"It helps that you're the size of a small bear," Sue said.

Dirk puffed up his chest. "Actually, I'm the size of a medium bear. Doc, I hear you are leaving us soon."

"Yeah, my contract is up, and it's time for me to move on. I just signed on for a four-month stint in San Diego."

"Be careful out there. They have earthquakes, fires, floods, and crazy Californians running around causing problems."

"Hopefully, it's safer than Phoenix. I hope I won't run into anyone more dangerous than Waverly. At least I don't have to worry about him anymore. He's gonna be locked up for the rest of his life."

"Technically, he already has been, since he was killed today in prison. Apparently his 180 pounds of narcissistic ego called out the wrong group. He was found beaten to death in his cell."

"Where'd you hear that?"

"Paramedics were talking about it. They got the call to pick up the body. They said it was a pretty bad scene, although the state might call it a suicide."

"Normally I would suggest a moment of silence for the fallen. I do hate the violence, but I'm glad he can't hurt anyone else."

"Sue, you're awfully quiet over there."

"I was just thinking about everything that happened. So much pain and loss was caused by one man, all for a little money. He could have just divorced her and taken half. Instead, six innocent people are dead, and the reputation of the hospital is stained forever. It may be time for me to move on, too. I might need a fresh start myself."

"Any idea where you want to go?"

"The mountains have always captured my attention, maybe Colorado or Utah."

"Nice places. How about you, Dirk. Any plans to move on?"

"Nope. I have a soccer league title to defend, a good job, and access to good food. Everything a growing boy needs to be happy."

"I hope you're finished growing. I propose a toast to us for ending the reign of terror unleashed by Waverly and managing to stay out of prison at the same time."

We clinked glasses and finished our late dinner on a more hopeful note. Outside, we said our goodbyes, and I breathed in the fresh, dry air.

"I'm gonna miss this place, Banshee. How about you? Are you ready for a new adventure?"

Banshee danced and swished his tail. He was always ready for new adventures.

ACKNOWLEDGEMENTS

For those of you looking for Tempe Memorial Hospital on a map, I will save you some time and disclose the hospital is fictional. Since we had murders and corruption raging through the hallways, I did not want to besmirch the reputation of a real hospital.

I have wanted to incorporate a dramatic death in the hospital for some time now, and the MRI scene fit the bill. MRI magnets are extremely powerful, and each year people are severely injured or killed when a metal object is inadvertently left in the exam area. A metal oxygen bottle becomes a deadly torpedo when the magnet is turned on. Although I have never heard of a box of nails left in an MRI suite, I imagine they would do the damage described in the opening scene.

This book also touches briefly on the issue of narcotic addiction among doctors. Unfortunately, it is a real issue as physicians have knowledge of the medications, access to them, and work in extremely stressful environments. Each state medical board has their own processes to help physicians suffering from drug addiction. If you, or a physician you know, need help, please reach out to the state medical board or some other entity for aid in recovery.

The odds of farmers brought to the emergency room by their wives having a serious illness approaches one hundred percent. Ask anyone with emergency room experience for a story about a farmer, and you won't be disappointed. Those dudes will have a pitchfork impaled through their thigh and ask for a couple of bandaids so they can get back to work.

A big shout out to all of my beta readers who found all of the errors I missed the first one hundred times I read through the manuscript – Cam Torrens, Niamh McAnally, Christy Burnett-Cooper, Gail Olmsted, Lucille Guarino, and Joe Lewis. All of them are talented writers themselves if you are looking for a new author to follow.

As always, I need to thank the entire team at Black Rose Writing. They may be a small press, but they are mighty, and together we sell a hell of a lot of books. A big thank you to Tamara, my wife and editor, who turns my clunky phrases into non-clunky phrases. She will hate that last sentence but I am not going to let her change it.

The final, and most important thank you, is to you, the readers. There are millions of books available, and I am constantly humbled at the number of people who choose to spend time with my books each day. Thank you for the support, and I will keep on writing new stories. Book seven is just getting started and will be based in San Diego, but I have no idea yet how it will turn out. Follow me on my website at garygerlacher.com to stay updated on the latest releases.

Stay safe out there, and check the MRI suite out before you start an exam.

ABOUT THE AUTHOR

Gary Gerlacher is a pediatric emergency physician who trained and worked in multiple Texas emergency rooms before opening his own pediatric urgent care clinics. His thirty years in medicine have focused on expanding access to high quality care for all children, and his stories give a unique view of the inner workings of the emergency room.

For fun, he runs a competitive cheer gym with his twin daughters, and he likes to golf and race cars. Gerlacher can be found eating cheese pizza most days of the week. He has three adult children and resides in Dallas with his two rescue dogs and his wife Tamara. Visit Garygerlacher.com to stay up to date on future books.

THE AJ DOCKER & BANSHEE THRILLER SERIES

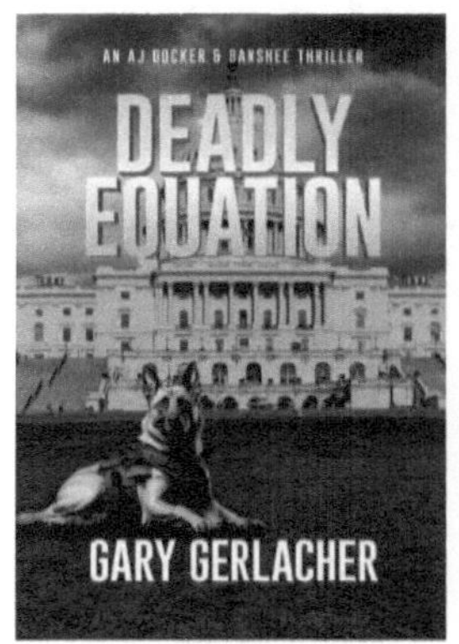

NOTE FROM GARY GERLACHER

Word-of-mouth is crucial for any author to succeed. If you enjoyed *Phantom Files*, please leave a review online—anywhere you are able. Even if it's just a sentence or two. It would make all the difference and would be very much appreciated.

Thanks!
Gary Gerlacher

We hope you enjoyed reading this title from:

www.blackrosewriting.com

Subscribe to our mailing list – *The Rosevine* – and receive **FREE** books, daily deals, and stay current with news about upcoming releases and our hottest authors.
Scan the QR code below to sign up.

Already a subscriber? Please accept a sincere thank you for being a fan of Black Rose Writing authors.

View other Black Rose Writing titles at
www.blackrosewriting.com/books and use promo code
PRINT to receive a **20% discount** when purchasing.